GHOST RIVER

AN EVANS NOVEL OF THE WEST

GHOST RIVER

L.J. WASHBURN

M. EVANS & COMPANY, INC.   NEW YORK

Library of Congress Cataloging-in-Publication Data

Washburn, L. J.

  Ghost river.
  (An Evans novel of the West)
  I. Title.   II. Series.
  PS3573.A787G4   1988   813'.54   88-28357
  ISBN 0-87131-556-4

M. Evans and Company, Inc.
216 East 49 Street
New York, New York 10017

Manufactured in the United States of America

9 8 7 6 5 4 3 2 1

*For Gabby, Lullaby,
Fuzzy, and Kerry*

Chapter One

The town of Grady was about as sun-blasted a place as Jacob Travers had ever seen. The buildings were dusty and bleached out, and from the looks of them, so were the inhabitants.

Travers didn't care about the people or the shabby frame buildings. His eye was on the large false-fronted structure that housed the Grady General Mercantile Emporium and Express Office.

As long as there was plenty of money there, Travers didn't care about anything else.

Emory Moore, who rode next to Travers, had done a good job of scouting the place. According to Emory, several of the local ranches had their payrolls waiting in the express office today, shipped in from their headquarters back east. They could be in and out in a hurry and ride off maybe fifteen, twenty thousand dollars richer.

Travers looked forward to having the money in his hands, where he could feel it and see it, and taste it if he had a mind to.

There were five of them. Travers and Emory rode just in front, with the other three men hanging back slightly. Sam, Lobo, and

Hankins were good on jobs like this: not overly bright, but willing to follow orders and handy with their guns. Travers hoped it wouldn't come to shooting, but if it did, he would feel better knowing that the three men were backing him up.

He was a young man with old eyes, lean-bodied and accustomed to long hours in the saddle. Brown hair hung down onto his shoulders. His brown denim pants and faded blue bib-front shirt were dusty and patched, and his black hat had seen a lot of wear. But the supple leather of his holster and shell belt and saddle said that he knew how to take care of the things that were important.

"How's it look to you?" Emory Moore asked as he reined in.

Travers glanced at him. Emory was his usual deceptive self. Travers and the others might look like the hardcases that they were, but Emory looked more like a big friendly farmer. The black hair under his hat was curly, and the wire-framed spectacles made his pale blue eyes look weak and hid the sparkle of a man who loved practical jokes. He was thick-waisted and gave an impression of slowness, both in body and mind.

But Travers had good reason to know just how quickly Emory could move, how ruthless and violent he could be when he had to. Emory had planned this job, as he had planned all their others. It would pay off; their robberies always did.

"Looks good," Travers replied softly. His eyes scanned the plank sidewalks. Nobody was paying much attention to them. Strangers in town on a Saturday were nothing unusual. Travers swung down from the saddle as Emory did likewise. They didn't have to look to know that the other three would be following their lead.

When the horses were tied up at the hitch rail, four of the men started strolling across the narrow alley that ran alongside the general store and express office. Hankins stayed behind to keep an eye on the horses and make sure nobody bothered them. Exuberant kids had been known to spook horses and really botch up a job.

There was a door down the sidewalk that opened directly into the express office. Instead of using it, Emory turned in at the entrance leading into the mercantile. Plenty of noise came from inside the store as Emory opened the door. He paused to let a middle-aged woman and two nearly grown girls step through the door in front of him. The girls cast their eyes toward Travers for a second, and one said something to the other in a whisper. They laughed.

Travers ignored them. He had barely noticed them in the first place.

He wished there were fewer people in the place. A crowd made it easier to blend in, but there was nothing worse than innocent people underfoot in a fight. Maybe it wouldn't turn out that way.

He followed Emory into the store, Sam and Lobo close behind him.

There were counters and stacks of goods everywhere, the aisles between crowded with customers and clerks. To the right, the arch that led into the express office was partially blocked by men leaning against the wall, chewing on pipes and talking. Emory smiled at the men and moved on into the express office, Travers at his side. Emory always had a friendly grin for everybody, Travers reflected fleetingly, even folks he was about to rob.

"Son of a bitch!" a voice said, suddenly strident. "I seen that feller's face on a wanted poster over in San Felipe!"

Travers tensed, glancing back over his shoulder. He saw one of the lounging ranch hands pointing a finger at Lobo. Lobo had only been with the bunch for six months and had sworn that he had never operated in this part of the country before, but he could've been lying.

Now, as the half-breed knocked his sombrero to the back of his head with one hand and grabbed for his gun with the other, Travers knew that he had been lying.

And that, coupled with his stupidity, might be the death of all of them.

"No!" Travers yelled, but he was too late and he knew it. The sleepy attitude of the men had vanished. All of them wore guns, and now they were reaching for them.

Emory spun around, his big hand flashing for his Colt. The pistol boomed at the same time as Lobo's, and two of the ranch hands were thrown back against the wall by the slugs. Travers looked at Emory as he made his own draw and saw the small shrug that the big man gave.

Bad luck came along sometimes, and there wasn't a damn thing a man could do about it.

The quarters were too close. As Travers's gun cleared its holster, a man grabbed at him. Travers lashed out, smacking the barrel against the cowboy's head. The man went down as Travers plowed into him, heading for the door to the sidewalk. Behind him, guns boomed.

"Dammit!"

Travers heard Emory's roar and swung around. Emory was staggering back against the counter with the barred window where a terrified clerk was cowering. The left sleeve of Emory's shirt was soaked with blood from a bullet wound. Emory lifted his right hand and fired, knocking down another of the men.

Somewhere the frightened express clerk found some courage and reached under the counter for a small pistol. Travers saw him past Emory's shoulder as he lifted the gun and pointed it at the back of the big man's head. At that range, even a small-caliber bullet would be fatal.

And Emory didn't see him, didn't know the man was back there.

Travers let instinct do the aiming for him. The Colt in his hand blasted a split-second later. The clerk screamed in pain and spun around, vanishing from sight as he flopped to the floor behind the counter.

On the wall behind him was a pattern of red where blood had splattered.

Emory's eyes met Travers's, but before Travers had a chance to read what was there, a fist punched him hard in the side. He staggered, the middle of his body going numb. He felt wet warmth on his leg and looked down to see the crimson flood going down his left side and soaking his pants.

The blow had been a bullet, not a fist. He was shot. He had just killed the clerk, and now he himself was shot. He was going to die in a little backwater town like Grady.

Travers let out a groan as he caught himself against the wall before he fell. The door was only a few steps away, but it seemed to take him an hour to get there. He forced his feet and legs to work, even though it seemed like they were no longer connected to the rest of him.

Somewhere along the way, the pistol slipped out of his fingers.

The gunfire seemed far away now, the shots echoing as if they were miles down a canyon. A hand clutched at Travers, but he pulled away from it somehow. A glance over his shoulder showed him the bullet-pocked figures of Sam and Lobo. They seemed to jump up and down slightly as slugs plowed into them. Then they pitched bonelessly to the floor.

Travers hit the door and was through it, half falling onto the sidewalk outside. Someone bumped him heavily, knocking him the rest of the way down. His face scraped the planks of the sidewalk.

He was not going to let himself be taken. They could shoot him down like a dog if they wanted to, but he was not going to let these people throw him in their jail and crow about how they had caught themselves a desperado.

Travers came up onto his hands and knees, got his feet under him, pushed himself into a crouching run.

He looked up and saw who had knocked him down. In his rush to get away, Emory Moore had bulled right past him, firing wildly.

"Emory!" Travers croaked. The numbness of the bullet wound was fading now, to be replaced by pure fire. "Help me!"

Emory didn't even look back. He snatched the reins of his horse from Hankins and vaulted into the saddle with an unusual grace for a man his size. Hankins was trying to get on his own mount, but the horse was skittish. The delay cost Hankins his life as several men poured out of the express office and opened fire on him. The bullets slammed him onto his back in the street.

The rest of the horses bolted.

Travers saw them coming toward him and knew he had to get out of the way or be trampled. He threw himself to the side and reached up at the same time, his fingers brushing the saddle of his own horse. Clutching desperately at the harness, he let himself be pulled along for a moment, then used all of his strength to grab the pommel and swing his legs up.

The thump as he landed in the saddle made his insides feel like they were being shredded. Travers shrieked in agony, but he stayed on top of the pounding animal.

Blinking back tears and gritting his teeth against the pain, he swiveled his head and looked for Emory. The leader of the gang was going in the other direction, riding south out of Grady. Several men were shooting at him with rifles, but Emory seemed untouched.

He was riding away, saving his own skin, and let the men he had brought here be damned.

Travers cried with more than pain. He had thought of Emory Moore as his friend, but Emory hadn't even taken the time to look back when Travers yelled for help.

As far as practical jokes went, it was one of Emory's best.

Of course, it didn't matter a whole hell of a lot now. Before much longer, Travers would be dead, and he knew it all too well.

Vaguely he heard bullets humming over his head. His horse was a good one, though, with plenty of sand and speed. None of the hayburners back in town could match him, Travers thought.

And that didn't matter either. He could outrun the pursuit, if there was one, but there was no getting away from death.

Every bound of the galloping horse sent fresh waves of pain racing through Travers. He felt his strength flowing out along with his blood, and as the horse left Grady behind, Travers slumped forward along the animal's neck. He dug his fingers into the horse's mane and hung on for dear life.

Dear life . . . His lips curved in a ghastly semblance of a grin. He had thought that life wasn't so dear, that there wasn't even a whole hell of a lot to live for. Until today, he had figured that he would be just about as well off dead as alive.

Funny how getting shot in the gut made a man look at things differently.

"Oh, God!" Jacob Travers screamed as a new surge of pain racked him. "God. . . ."

Funny as all hell.

Chapter Two

After a while Travers was barely aware of what was happening around him. The pain faded and the numbness came back, bringing with it a penetrating cold that was all the stronger for the late afternoon heat. Travers may have seen the rugged terrain with its scrubby vegetation through his slitted eyes, but his brain took no notice of it.

Several men from Grady chased him, but as the big black horse he rode thundered on into the west, the pursuers gradually dropped back and finally gave it up. After all, the would-be robbers had never even gotten their holdup under way. It had been a failure all the way around.

A failure—somewhere in Travers's brain, he told himself he was exactly that. He had never succeeded in one damn thing he had tried, not in the long run. For a while he had been an owlhoot, but now even that had come to a bad end.

The horse ran on toward the setting sun, the rider swaying and bobbing on its back, hanging on with fingers that were now cramped into claws.

It was hard to believe that only two years had passed since he had started on the trail that led him here. . . .

Polly Dawes wasn't the prettiest girl he had ever seen, not by a long shot. In fact, she was about as plain as a mud fence except for the massive bosoms thrusting out from her chest. But after she kissed him the first time, Jacob Travers knew he would do any damn thing she wanted.

"Now that's enough, Jacob," she said, pressing her hands against his shirt. "We'd better get back inside before someone misses us."

They were standing in deep shadows next to the church where the Reverend Malachi Travers conducted services. Tonight, the church wasn't being used for preaching, but rather the whole community had come together for a covered-dish supper.

He let her go as she gently pushed away from him. In the moonlight he saw the smile that curved her full lips. She reached up and ran her fingers through her long, dark hair, arching her back and making him all too aware of the lush curves of her body.

"My lands," she said softly, "you certainly can kiss for a preacher's boy, Jacob."

"Polly," he said, his voice slightly hoarse. "Are you sure I shouldn't ought to kiss you again?"

Her smile took on a strange cast, and he wished he could see her eyes better in the shadows. "Why, you're just full of the devil, aren't you? What would your father say if he saw you out here sparking a hussy like me?"

Jacob swallowed and then licked dry lips. "I don't care what my pa says. I just know what I want."

"You mean you'd defy your father?" There was a breathlessness in Polly's whisper.

"Hell, yes." Even as he said the words, something inside Jacob cringed. But he said them anyway, and his jaw tightened with the depth of his feelings.

Polly suddenly leaned against him, taking him by surprise, and her lips again found his. She kissed him hard, the wet heat of her mouth making his knees threaten to buckle for a second.

She pulled back enough to say, "I believe you'd dare anything, Jacob Travers! Would you ride Colonel Jeb Stuart?"

Jacob's eyes widened. She was talking about her uncle's prize stallion, and he had made it plain that he would shoot anyone who bothered Colonel Jeb Stuart. Leander Dawes had served under the famous commander, and he had named the fastest animal in two states after the man in honor of Stuart's lightning-quick strikes.

Now, even with Polly Dawes soft and warm and inviting in his arms, Jacob had the sense to hesitate.

She leaned closer against him. Her lips trailed over the line of his jaw and then moved down to his throat. "Please."

Lordy! Jacob felt himself blushing hotly. Maybe she was right about being a hussy after all. She surely did know how to bend a fellow around to her way of thinking.

"All right," he said abruptly. "If you want me to ride Colonel Jeb Stuart, I'll do it."

She kissed him again, long and hungrily. "I knew you would," she whispered when she pulled away. "I just knew it."

Travers felt himself falling from the saddle, but he couldn't do anything to stop himself. The fire in his side came roaring back when he landed hard on the ground. He curled up and fought the pain, his teeth clamping down on his lip and biting right through it. His mouth started to fill up with blood.

When the flames in his body subsided, he was able to raise his head and look around. The world was dark and blurry, and he knew the sun had set. Far above him were quivering pinpoints of light that he knew had to be stars.

A few feet away, munching peacefully on a tuft of grass, was his horse.

At least he had something to be thankful for. If the horse had run off, he really would be in bad shape.

Travers grinned hideously. As if he could be any worse off than he was now. . . . All his luck had finally run out. There was no help for him now, no reason to keep going.

No reason not to.

He climbed to his feet. It took almost fifteen minutes, but then he was back up. Clutching his left arm across his middle, he lurched after the horse, reaching for it with his right. The animal shied away at first, but then it responded to Travers's hoarse whispers. He had no strength to pull himself into the saddle. He grasped the stirrup and simply stood there, breathing raggedly.

With Polly at his side, he led Colonel Jeb Stuart out of the stable. As the moonlight washed over them, he felt a fresh tingle of nervousness. If Leander Dawes happened to be looking in this direction, there was no way he could miss seeing them.

There was no alarm from the ranch house. Quickly, Jacob led the horse around the stable and out of sight. With Polly's soft, triumphant laughter ringing in his ears, he swung a leg over the animal's back and hauled himself up.

"What a noble sight! Now ride him, Jacob. Ride him!"

Jacob grinned down at her, feeling reckless and romantic, and said, "Ride with me."

Polly shook her head. The moonlight struck silver glints off her raven hair. "I'd rather watch you," she said.

Jacob nodded, still grinning, flushed with exuberance at the daring of what they were doing. His heels dug into the animal's side, he gave a low urging cry, and with a surging bound, Colonel Jeb Stuart was off.

The fields behind the stable were flat and unobstructed. There was nothing to slow down the horse as it ran. Wind washed over Jacob's face as he leaned forward, wrapping his fingers in the Colonel's mane and establishing the silent line of communication that existed only between the best horses and the best riders.

The stars overhead seemed to blur, the horse galloped so fast.

Jacob let out a whoop. He couldn't help it. God, he was so happy right at this moment! A wonderful horse under him, the night wind in his face, a girl waiting for him when the ride was done. . . .

No man could want more.

The explosion of the shotgun followed Polly's scream by less than a second.

Travers didn't know when he had gotten back in the saddle, but he slowly became aware that he was riding again. He was fading in and out of consciousness, the memories of his past seeming more real than what was actually happening to him.

A part of his mind was still coherent enough to realize that he was about to die.

Something cool touched his face.

Travers raised his head and blinked. Tendrils of fog brushed his skin. What the hell was fog doing out here in this wasteland?

And then he saw that it was coming from the river.

Travers blinked and weakly reined in the horse. Several yards ahead of him, the ground began to slope down, and he heard the soft, unmistakable gurgle of running water.

Some clouds had obscured the moon for a moment, but they moved on, letting the lambent glow illuminate what was in front of Travers. The light was reflected back by the slowly moving current of the river. More fog eddied over the water.

Travers shook his head. He had never been through this part of the territory, but he had seen all the maps, talked to plenty of people who had passed this way.

And there was not supposed to be a river here.

No one had ever mentioned such a thing to him. It was not on any of the maps. But there it was.

"Reckon I'm seeing things," Travers muttered through dry, cracked lips. He couldn't remember when he had last had a drink.

Suddenly it was important to him to make sure he wasn't imagining the stream. He started to get down from the horse, lost his balance, and half fell out of the saddle. He caught himself before he sprawled on the ground, took a deep breath, and made his feet work.

Travers walked into the edge of the water. It was there, all right, and not a delusion. Carefully, he sank to his knees. The sudden thirst that was gripping him made him want to throw himself forward and gulp down the cold water, but he knew if he did he was liable to collapse and not be able to get back up.

It'd be a hell of a thing to drown here on the edge of the desert, he thought. He used his hand to scoop up water and splash it in his face. The drops that went in his mouth were cold and clean and without a doubt the best water he had ever tasted.

Strength seemed to flow back into him.

He came to his feet and looked around, saw the horse drinking a few feet away. It had been a long, hot run from Grady, and he couldn't let the horse suck down too much water. Travers splashed over to him and caught the reins, pulling him away from the stream.

Standing on the gentle bank, Travers tried to look across the river. It didn't seem like it should be too wide—most of the rivers and creeks in the territory were pretty narrow except when flash floods hit—but somehow he couldn't see the other side. And there was a fairly strong current as well, not to mention the fog.

Travers shook his head. He wasn't going to try to cross the river, not in his condition. But he wasn't going to leave it, either. A man didn't walk away from water like this, not in this always-dry country.

He was still convinced he was going to die, but maybe he could make a camp, wait for the end in relative comfort.

But if he did, the posse from Grady might catch up to him. He didn't want that.

The horse needed rest, too. It had made a valiant effort today. Travers held the reins and turned toward the south. He began plodding along the bank, leading the horse. Every step was painful, but something kept him moving.

It took Jacob a frantic few moments to realize that no one was shooting at him. Old Leander Dawes valued the horse too much to cut loose in his direction with a load of buckshot. Instead, the rancher was firing the shotgun into the air, summoning help.

Jacob saw men pouring out of the bunkhouse and knew he was in bad trouble. He whirled the horse around and banged his boots against its flanks, kicking it into a gallop.

If he could get far enough away from the pursuit, he was thinking, he could let the horse go and slip away on foot. He didn't think Dawes or his men would keep chasing him once they had the Colonel back.

The horse was running beautifully beneath him, its muscles working in an oh-so-smooth demonstration of pure speed and power. They weren't going to catch him tonight. No way in hell.

The Colonel stepped in a hole.

The horse screamed, and so did Jacob. Even if he had been using a saddle and stirrups, he wouldn't have been able to stay on the back of the cartwheeling animal. Jacob kept yelling as he flew through the air, his cry cut off suddenly as he slammed into the ground.

"On your feet, you hoss-thievin' son of a bitch!" one of hands snapped at him.

Jacob looked fearfully at the circle of men surrounding him. They all had guns out and were ready to use them.

"I wasn't stealing the horse—" he began.

One of the men stepped behind him and slammed the barrel of his gun against Jacob's shoulders. He yelped in pain and fell forward, catching himself with his hands. A booted foot kicked him, knocking him the rest of the way down.

"Now get back up and keep your goddamn mouth shut, boy," the first man ordered.

Jacob did as he was told this time.

They marched him across the field, leaving a man behind to see to the injured horse. Leander Dawes was waiting, and Jacob could see his face in the moonlight. He wished he couldn't. The rancher's bearded countenance, filled with fury, looked just like the image of a vengeful God that Jacob's father always summoned up in his sermons. Dawes's fingers dug cruelly into the flesh of Polly's arm, and she was weeping brokenly.

"Hush up, girl!" he barked at her. "If you're tellin' me the truth, you've got no reason to cry."

"It–it's the truth, Uncle Leander," Polly sobbed. "I swear it is. He made me bring him out here!"

Jacob heard the words as the ranch hands prodded him in front of Dawes, and he felt a coldness trickle down his spine.

Dawes ignored him for the moment and asked one of the hands, "What about Colonel Jeb Stuart?"

The cowboy replied, "His leg weren't broke, Mr. Dawes, but it looked like he damaged it right good."

"Thievin' young scalawag!" he snarled. "I'd be justified in cuttin' you right in half with this here greener, boy. You know that, don't you?"

Jacob took a deep breath. "I didn't steal—"

Dawes didn't let him get any farther. "Don't lie to me! And you a preacher's boy, on top of everything else."

"We ain't lynched a hoss thief in a long time," one of the ranch hands put in.

Polly clutched at her uncle's arm. "No, Uncle Leander, please don't kill him! I . . . I know he did wrong, but you don't have to kill him."

Jacob stared long and hard at her, but she wouldn't meet his eyes. He wasn't sure what-all she had told her uncle, but it had obviously been a long way from the truth.

Dawes sighed grudgingly. "Reckon we are supposed to have law and order out here now," he growled. "I'll turn you over to the sheriff."

Jacob had to ask. He looked at Polly and said, "What did you tell him?"

Dawes didn't let his niece answer. "Told me the truth, she did. Told me how you forced her to leave the church supper and bring you out here. Said you forced her to show you where the Colonel was kept. Threatened to hurt her if she didn't go along with you. You're a mighty sorry excuse for a human being, boy."

The rancher's face was like granite as he shouldered past Jacob and started across the field to see to his prized possession.

Jacob looked at the girl again and said, "Polly, how can you do this to me?"

"I . . . I don't know what you're talking about, Jacob," Polly said, still sobbing slightly. With one of the cries catching in her throat, she turned and ran toward the ranch house.

"Gal's had nothin' but bad luck where that hoss is concerned," one of the cowboys commented quietly. "First the boss gives her that chewin' out yesterday when she tried to ride the Colonel 'thout askin' him, and now this bastard uses her to try to steal the damned horse. Yep, bad luck all around."

That was surely true, Jacob thought. And all of it had wound up on his head.

Stumbling along beside the river, the horse's reins held tightly in his bloodstained hand, Travers could almost hear that clang of bars again. Two years and miles and miles of dusty trails, and he could still hear it.

Could still feel the pain of being shut up like that.

Never again. He'd keep going until he dropped, but he wouldn't be put in jail again.

He had seen the light in front of him for almost a minute before he realized what it was.

Then he stopped in his tracks and stared. Maybe a quarter of a mile away, a small spot of light shone against the blackness of the night. He couldn't be sure what it was, but it looked like lanternlight through the window of a building.

Could there be a farm or a ranch out here in the middle of nowhere? Someplace he could get help?

His mouth twisted wryly. Who would help a bloody, beat-down owlhoot? Nobody, that's who. And he had lost his gun back there in Grady, so he couldn't even force whoever lived up there beside the river to give him a hand.

Still, the light was in his path, and he was stubborn enough that he wasn't going to change the way he was going. He growled, "Come on, horse," and started walking again.

Every step seemed to drain more strength from him. He wished he had the energy to drink some more water from the river, but now even that seemed like too much of an effort. All he could do was keep putting one foot in front of the other. He watched the speck of light grow as he approached. It was a window, all right, and now he could see a good-sized wooden building that went with it. In the moonlight, it was a sturdy-looking structure, built close by the river. When he got within fifty feet of it, he could see a sign hanging over the long porch that fronted it, but he couldn't make out the words painted there.

There was a hitch rack in front of the place, but Travers didn't bother tying up the horse. The animal wasn't going anywhere, and it wouldn't really matter if he did.

Three steps led up onto the porch. Travers climbed them with the last vestige of strength in his wounded body. His boots clomped on the wide planks of the porch, and he clenched his fingers into a weak fist. He banged it against the door once, then had to slump against the panel. He was going to pass out at any second, and he knew it.

"Help me," he murmured.

The door opened.

Travers felt himself falling forward. Strong arms caught him before he could hit the floor inside, and lowered him gently. His eyes were closed, but he pried them open.

And looked up into the dirty, whiskered face of an old man with tobacco juice dribbling out of his toothless mouth.

"Say, younker, 'pears you could use a hand."

The old man extended a gnarled, callused paw. Travers's insides were on fire again, and it was all he could do to lift his arm.

He took the old man's hand, and then knew nothing more.

Chapter Three

Travers's father was standing before him, holding the thick black Bible he always carried. There was an ominous frown on his broad, freckled face. Light from the candle on the table beside the bed shone on his bald scalp.

Slowly, Reverend Travers raised his left hand and pointed a shaking finger at his wounded son. He raised his thunderous voice and intoned solemnly, condemningly, "Murderer!"

Travers cringed at the sight and sound. For as far back as he could remember, his father had been telling him how sinful he was, how the Lord would punish him for all the things he was feeling and doing.

Now it looked like his father was right. If the pain in Travers's belly was any indication, he was suffering plenty of righteous wrath.

He deserved it; he knew that. Back in Grady, he had killed that clerk who was about to shoot Emory. Up until that moment, there might have been hope for him. Even though he had been on the outlaw trail for a couple of years, he had never killed anybody.

He'd busted a few skulls in saloon fights and stole more than his share, but he'd never taken a life.

Now it was too late. Like the vision of his father said, he was a murderer.

Travers knew he was imagining the tall, stern-faced man in front of him. He was coherent enough to realize that he was in a bed somewhere. He ran his hands down over his body and felt the bandages wrapped tightly around his middle.

"Heathen idolator! Fornicator!"

Travers tried to ignore the charges that his father was leveling at him. He decided the figure wasn't a ghost, since his father was still alive to the best of his knowledge. Instead, it was his own guilt talking to him, letting him know just what a sorry specimen he really was.

Hell, that wasn't anything new. Travers had known that for a long time, ever since he had chosen the easy way out whenever he was faced with a problem.

Like being stuck in a hoosegow for something he hadn't really done.

"What's going to happen to me, Sheriff?" Jacob asked, his hands clutching the bars of the cell door.

The sheriff shrugged his heavy shoulders. "Hell, I reckon you'll stand trial and be found guilty of whatever Mr. Dawes wants you charged with. Then you'll probably be sent off to the territorial prison for ten or twelve years."

Jacob swallowed the terrified sob that wanted to come out of his throat. "Even if I'm not guilty?"

"Now who do you 'spose a jury in this county's goin' to believe, son, you or Leander Dawes?"

Jacob knew the answer to that question.

He sank down on the hard bunk and let his head drop into his hands. Outside the barred window, the night was quiet. It was hard to believe this was the same night that had begun with him asking Polly Dawes to slip outside the church with him during the covered-dish supper.

A bitter taste rose in his mouth at the thought of Polly. He could see plainly now that she had used him to get back at her uncle. She had gotten in trouble for trying to ride Colonel Jeb Stuart, so she had decided to flout Dawes's authority by getting someone else to ride the treasured horse.

He had just been unlucky enough to be the one she chose.

Now he was facing what seemed like a lifetime in prison just because he had wanted to kiss a girl with big bosoms.

It wasn't fair. It just wasn't fair at all.

He was staring at the floor of the cell and didn't even know he had a visitor until his father's voice boomed out, "Seek ye the face of Satan? Then look ye in the smile of a woman!"

Jacob closed his eyes and let his head droop even more for a moment. When at last he looked up to see his father standing there on the other side of the bars with a pained, sanctimonious expression on his face, Jacob could no longer control his anger.

He came up off the bunk and lunged toward the door, his hands reaching through the bars. His father jerked back out of reach, startled by Jacob's abrupt violence.

"You pious old bastard!" Jacob shouted at him. "Can't you see I'm in trouble? Can't you help me?"

Reverend Travers shook his head. "Only God can help you now, you evil child. Turn to Him, and perhaps in His infinite mercy He will take pity on even a wretched soul like yours."

"Wretched soul?" Jacob's voice shook with frustration. "I'm your *son!* Can't you help me?"

Again the shake of the head. "No son of mine is a horse thief."

"I didn't steal the damn horse! I was just riding it. Polly Dawes asked me to. It was all her idea!"

The sheriff said from the doorway leading into the cell block, "Here now, let's keep all that hollerin' down. Your pa's been good enough to come see you, boy, even though you've shamed him. You hadn't ought to yell at him. And it ain't goin' to help you none to try to blame what you did on a sweet little gal like Polly Dawes."

Suddenly Jacob slumped against the bars, all his energy gone.

"None of you believe me," he muttered. "Nobody gives a damn what I say. Maybe Dawes and his men should've lynched me. It would've saved some time."

"There's no necktie parties in my county," the sheriff said. "You just remember that. And settle down." He went back out into the office again.

Reverend Travers moved closer to the bars once more. He extended the thick black book he held. "Here, boy," he said. "Perhaps if you read this, you'll see how evil you are."

Jacob reached out, took the Bible from his father's hands, grimaced, and threw it back in his face. The minister ducked, the Bible bouncing off his upflung arm.

"Get the hell away from me," Jacob snarled. "I don't care if I ever see you again, old man, you understand that? You aren't my pa anymore. I'm not sure you ever really were."

Reverend Travers sighed and bent down to pick up the Bible. The binding had torn slightly when it hit the floor. "You have desecrated the word of God," he intoned. "I will pray for you, but I fear it will do little good."

He turned and slowly walked out of the cell block.

Jacob went back to his bunk. The encounter had left him with a bad taste in his mouth and an empty feeling in his middle. He and his father had never been close, but now it was like something had been ripped out of him, leaving a hole that hurt. For the first time in his life, he had really needed his father, and the old man had turned his back on him, wrapping himself in righteousness instead of helping.

There was only one person who could help him, Jacob realized. Himself.

And no matter what it took, he wasn't going to prison.

"Feelin' a mite better, air ye?"

Travers looked up to see the old man standing in the doorway of the little room. The old man was wearing grimy bib overalls, a flannel shirt, and an apron that had once been white but was now a mixture of various stains. He was carrying a steaming pot of something that smelled like stew.

At first whiff, the aroma coming from the pot was delicious to Travers and reminded him how long it had been since he had eaten. But then his stomach rebelled at the thought, cramping and making beads of sweat pop out on his forehead.

"Wh–Who the hell . . . are you . . . old man?"

"Reckon ya c'n call me George. It's my name, after all." The old-timer hefted the pot. "Reckon ya could do with some prairie dog stew?"

Travers moaned and closed his eyes, letting his head loll to the side on the thin, uncomfortable pillow. If he ignored the old coot, maybe he'd go away.

Still, someone had brought him in here and bandaged his wound, and there was only one likely candidate for that honor. Travers made himself open his eyes and sit up slightly. "I guess you saved my life," he said. "Thanks."

George waved a hand. "No thanks necessary. I'd'a done the same for nearly anybody . . . even fellers who ain't so durned persnickety 'bout my cookin'."

It looked like Travers was going to have to eat some of the stew to avoid hurting the old man's feelings. He said, "All right. I suppose I could do with a bowl."

"Figgered you'd see it that way. This here concoction's plumb good for ya, it is. You'll see."

Travers remembered thinking while he was heading for this place that no one in his right mind would help him. It appeared that he had been right. This old man had probably been out here by himself for so long that he was touched in the head.

George spooned out some of the prairie dog stew into a battered tin bowl and handed it to Travers along with a spoon. Travers raised himself into a sitting position, finding the maneuver surprisingly easy. His wound didn't pain him nearly as much as he had expected it to.

The stew, when he finally dug into it, wasn't bad, either. As he ate, George gestured at the bandages and said, "Looks like you run into a heap o' trouble on your way here, son."

Travers gave a brief shake of his head. "I wasn't heading for this place."

"Shoot, ever'body comes to Ghost River sooner or later," George said with a raucous laugh. "Ain't no other way through this part o' the country."

"Ghost River? I never heard of it."

"You walked right along beside it for quite a spell, son. That's what led you here."

Travers looked around at the bare wood of the walls. The room was narrow and unfurnished except for the bed. "What is this, some kind of inn?"

"This here's the Ghost River Tradin' Post. Now don't tell me you never heard of that, neither."

Travers shook his head. "I'm afraid I haven't. You been out here long?"

George grinned and shook his head. "Longer'n you'd believe if I told you, boy."

Travers scraped up the last of the stew and then handed the empty bowl to the old man. He was still expecting his stomach to rebel at any moment and force the food back up, but so far it seemed to be settling down. He was feeling stronger again, just like he had after drinking the water from Ghost River.

He wondered why he had never seen the stream marked on any maps or heard anybody talking about it. As important as water was in these parts, you'd think that a river with such clear, cold water would be well-known.

He felt George watching him with intense dark eyes and remembered that the old man had asked him a question. Well, George had taken care of him and fed him. Travers supposed he deserved an answer.

"I ran into some trouble, all right," he said. "And I reckon I caused a lot of it, too." The guilt over the clerk's killing came back to him, not as sharp as the pain of the bullet wound, but somehow striking deeper within him. "You might not want to help me anymore when I tell you about it. You see, there was a robbery back in Grady, and a fellow got killed. . . ."

George shook his head. "Don't recollect askin' for all the details, younker. You can tell me 'bout it later, if you've a mind to. Right now we'd best worry 'bout that hole in your innards. I got me a few old-fashioned remedies that ought to fix you right up."

"Old-fashioned remedies, eh? Been in the family a long time?"

"Longer'n you'd believe—"

"—if you told me. I know." Travers let his eyes close as a wave of sleepiness washed over him again. He supposed it was the full belly making him weary. That and the ordeal he had gone through, of course.

Well, if George didn't want to hear about the would-be robbery and the killing, that was all right, Travers supposed. He had decided to make a clean breast of the business so that the old man could boot him out of here if he wanted to, but Travers knew damn well he was in no shape to turn down any assistance he could get.

He'd sleep awhile, he told himself, gather a little more strength, then face whatever the future held for him.

Jacob had dozed off in the jail cell, sleeping fitfully until the sky in the barred window began to turn gray with approaching dawn. Then he couldn't stand the hard bunk anymore and got up to pace back and forth in the narrow confines of the cell. He stopped for a few minutes to eat the breakfast the sheriff brought him, although he didn't taste any of it, then resumed his nervous pacing.

The lawman just looked at him and shook his head. He had seen prisoners react like that before, like wild animals that had been stuck in a cage, and he knew it wasn't good.

Jacob was still at his pacing when the sheriff brought another visitor at midmorning. But he stopped short when he saw Polly Dawes staring mournfully through the bars at him.

"What the hell are you doing here?" he demanded.

"You just stop that stuff, kid," the sheriff warned. "You treat Miss Dawes decent. She don't have to be here, you know."

"Why are you here?" Jacob asked her, ignoring the lawman. Polly lifted her chin. Her face was set in tight lines. "I came to see if there was anything I could do for you, Jacob. Just because you . . . did what you did . . . doesn't mean I can't forgive you."

"You forgive me?" He laughed shortly. "Well, that's mighty good to hear. You don't know how I worried about that very thing last night."

Her eyes showed a fleeting reaction to the bitterness in his voice, but it was gone in an instant and no one except Jacob could have seen it and recognized it for what it was. Polly said, "Very well, if that's the way you feel, I don't suppose I can help you." She started to turn away.

"Polly!"

She stopped and looked over her shoulder at him. "Yes?"

"If you really want to help me," he said earnestly, "you could tell your uncle and the sheriff here the truth about what really happened last night." He knew it was hopeless, but he had to make the effort.

"Why, I don't understand, Jacob. I've already told everyone exactly what happened."

He nodded slowly. "I figured that's what you'd say. So long, Polly. I don't want you coming around anymore."

She sniffed. "Good-bye, Jacob."

Then she was gone, and he couldn't help but laugh. To him, she was so transparent, but she had everybody else fooled.

The sheriff stood in the cell-block door, shaking his head. "You don't have the sense the good Lord gave you, son," he said. "If that little gal had put in a good word for you, it might've made her uncle go easier on you."

"I don't want her help, Sheriff, it's as simple as that."

The sheriff shrugged. "Your funeral, boy."

Jacob resumed his pacing. He got the routine down—four steps, turn, four steps, turn. It got pretty damned monotonous in a hurry, but when the sheriff brought his lunch, the man didn't see anything unusual in the way Jacob turned toward him as he unlocked the door. The sheriff stepped inside to put the tray on the bunk when Jacob lunged at him. There hadn't been any prisoners in this jail for a long time except cowboys sleeping off a drunken binge and an occasional petty thief. He wasn't expecting trouble.

"Hey!" the sheriff yelled. Jacob crashed into him, the lunch tray going onto the floor with a clatter. The collision staggered both of them.

The sheriff grabbed for his gun, but Jacob's hand was there first. Jacob yanked the Colt out and used all the strength that desperation gave him to slap the weapon across the sheriff's head. The lawman's hat broke the force of the blow somewhat, but there was enough behind it to knock the sheriff to his knees. He moaned and reached for his head.

Jacob planted a foot in the man's chest and shoved hard, knocking the sheriff back against the bunk. Leveling the gun at him and earing back the hammer, Jacob said nervously, "Now you just be still, Sheriff! Don't move!"

The sheriff groaned and kept massaging the sore lump that was springing up on his head. "What the hell are you doin', boy?" he demanded.

"I'm breaking out of jail, Sheriff." Jacob laughed, trying to hold down the anxiety that was making his insides jump around crazily. "Didn't anybody ever break out of this cracker box before?"

"Not since I been sheriff." The lawman held out a hand. "Now, why don't you just give me that gun back, and I won't say nothing about this little stunt, boy. I know you're scared of goin' to prison. But this ain't goin' to help your case."

Jacob shook his head. "No, Sheriff, I'm leaving. There's nothing for me around here anymore."

The truth of that statement sank in on him. His father was the only family he had left, and he didn't care if he ever saw that old hypocrite again. And he sure wasn't going to hang around because of Polly Dawes.

The sheriff started to get up, then sank back when Jacob gestured sharply with the gun. "I'm in enough trouble already, Sheriff," Jacob told him. "I don't reckon shooting you would make things any worse."

"You're no killer, son. I can tell that. Give it up."

Jacob backed to the open door of the cell. "Forget it, Sheriff." He stepped out and slammed the door behind him. "I'm leaving."

"I'll raise a ruckus soon's you do, Jacob. You won't make it to the town limits."

"You won't do anything if I shoot you." Even as he said it, Jacob knew he couldn't do that, but maybe the threat would be sufficient.

The sheriff grinned wryly. "A gunshot'd draw even more attention than me yellin'."

Jacob realized he was right, and the feeling of being trapped came back to him. Maybe the sheriff was right. Maybe this escape attempt was just going to make things worse.

What he needed was something to draw attention away from the jail. There was a kerosene lantern on the sheriff's desk, Jacob remembered, and a field of fairly dry grass out back.

It took only a second to raise the chimney and get the wick lit. Then Jacob ran to the back door of the jail and jerked it open. A narrow alley ran behind the row of buildings, and the field was beyond it. He flung the lantern out into the grass as far as he could.

It burst with a tinkle of glass, and the dry vegetation caught fire almost immediately. Flames shot up with a whoosh, racing along the alley.

There wasn't much wind, and Jacob felt sure the blaze wouldn't leap the alley and set the town on fire. But the threat of that would be enough to occupy the citizens. If they were busy fighting the fire, they wouldn't be chasing him.

He ducked around the corner of the jail, still hearing the sheriff's cries from inside. Behind him, billows of smoke began rolling upward into the clear blue sky.

Jacob ran into the main street, his eyes darting from side to side. His gaze lit on several horses hitched at a rack in front of the building next to the jail.

They had called him a horse thief, he thought. Hell, he might as well be one.

He yanked loose the reins of the best-looking mount and leaped into the saddle. People were pouring out of the buildings now as the cry of "Fire!" began to ring through the town. One man spotted Jacob and yelled, "Hey! That's my horse!"

The man pulled his gun and let go a blast in Jacob's direction. Jacob heard the bullet smack through the air close by his head, and he leaned over the horse's neck to present a smaller target. He kicked the horse into motion and let out a yell as it broke into a gallop down the street.

He thought several more men took shots at him, but he could never be sure. All he knew for certain was that nobody hit him. Torn by the desire to catch him and the need to keep their homes and businesses from burning down, the townspeople did the only thing they could.

They let him go.

The horse was a good one, carrying him out of town within moments. There was no pursuit, and as he headed out on the prairie and left the settlement behind him, he glanced back over his shoulder and saw the smoke that marked his departure.

They wouldn't ever forget Jacob Travers around here, he thought proudly. He wasn't just a gawky preacher's boy anymore, no sir. He had busted out of that jail just like a genuine desperado.

And from now on, he vowed, the wind of his escape buffeting his face, that was just what he would be.

He had stayed on that course for long months, stealing only what he needed to survive at first, gradually putting together an outfit. His horse and his saddle and his gun were the most important things he stole. As long as he had them, he could go where he pleased and take what he wanted.

He discovered that he had a natural talent with the Colt that now rode on his hip. There were faster men, he was sure, but he practiced for long hours and was still improving. And there were few more accurate, he thought, taking pride in his skill.

When he met up with Emory Moore in a Tascosa saloon, Emory had agreed with that assessment. He had seen how good with a gun Travers was when he introduced Sam and Hankins as federal marshals, not expecting Travers to draw on them and try to escape. There would have been some shooting that day if Emory hadn't grabbed Travers's gun hand and explained quickly that it had all been a joke. Emory had soothed the ruffled feelings of Sam and Hankins, and Travers had been accepted into the band.

Travers had proved to be a worthy member of the gang. It hadn't taken Emory long to discover that Travers was more intelligent than Sam or Hankins. Travers took to being second in command with no trouble.

They rode together, pulled jobs when they needed to, and got roaring drunk and chased whores when the law wasn't on their trail. Emory had a great fondness for jokes, and Travers had been the butt of a few of them, although Emory tended to pull most of his pranks on Sam and Hankins, and Lobo when he had joined up later. All in all, it hadn't been a bad way to live.

And that was the way things had stayed until the job in Grady had gone sour right from the start.

Now, as he lay in the bed and dozed, Travers realized what a fool he had been to ever trust Emory Moore. He had looked on Emory almost as a friend, as much of a friend as any outlaw could ever have. And Emory had repaid that friendship by running out on him.

Travers wasn't sure anymore that he was going to die from the bullet he had taken, but he knew it was only a matter of time now until he wound up in jail. The posse from Grady would follow his tracks right to Ghost River. When they showed up here, the old man would turn him over. George wouldn't have a choice.

Anyway, when he found out that Travers was a killer, he

wouldn't want to help him. Like anybody decent, he'd want the filthy murderer out from under his roof.

Travers closed his eyes and burrowed deeper into the pillow. Maybe finding this run-down trading post hadn't been so lucky after all.

Maybe Ghost River was just one more stop on his trail to hell.

Chapter Four

Travers lost track of time. For the most part, he slept, and when he awoke, the old man called George was there with some more of his prairie dog stew. Travers was never sure just what was in the concoction, although he doubted it was really made from prairie dogs. Whatever was in it, it was making his strength come back to him in a hurry. After what seemed like only a couple of nights, the wound in his belly felt like it was almost healed. He had noticed upon awakening several times that the bandages had been changed, and he was surprised that the old man was able to do that without disturbing him. Evidently he was using that old family remedy on the wound when he changed the dressings.

As early morning sunlight shone through the single window in the little room, Travers decided to test his legs. He sat up, felt a slight touch of dizziness for a second, and then swung his feet off the bunk. Carefully, he stood up.

At first the floor seemed to tilt underneath him, and he thought he was going to pitch forward onto his face. But then things settled down, and he was able to take a deep breath and a tentative step.

The door opened. George poked his whiskered face through and grinned broadly when he saw Travers on his feet. "Feelin' a mite feisty, air ye? That there's a good sign, son."

"Just thought I'd see if I could walk yet. I don't want to hang around here and be a burden to you."

"No burden for me. Shoot, you ain't been near as much trouble as some o' the sidewinders who've come to Ghost River. Some o' them was in such bad shape I really had to work on 'em."

One of the stories Travers's father had used in his sermons came back to him. "Regular Good Samaritan, aren't you?" he grunted.

"Never thought o' myself that way. Way I sees it, I'm just doin' what I can to he'p folks get where they's goin'."

"Well, I appreciate what you've done for me," Travers said sincerely. He glanced around the room. "Where the hell are my clothes?" He was wearing only the bottom half of his long johns and the bandages wrapped around his middle, and he was starting to feel good enough that the lack of clothes bothered him.

George jerked a dirty thumb at the big main room of the trading post behind him. "I done cleaned 'em up for ya. Them blood-stains was a woolly booger to get out, lemme tell ya. But they're clean again." There was pride in the old man's voice as he went on, "Ain't run acrost too many things I couldn't get clean."

"Well, you're a right industrious fellow, George," Travers grinned. "How about fetching them for me?"

George shook his head. "You may be able to get up out'n that there bed, but you ain't in no shape to go gallivantin' nowheres else. You just rest a mite longer."

"I could go get my clothes myself," Travers pointed out.

"Reckon you could . . . if you was that teched in the head as to try."

Travers snorted. He was a better judge of how he felt than some old desert rat running a trading post. He took a step toward the door—

George caught him before he fell, strong hands clamping on to Travers's arm and holding him up. "What'd I tell ya?" the old man demanded. "You ain't got no more strength'n a little cat yet, son. It just seems like you're better compared to how sick you was before. Now get back in bed, why don't you, and get some more rest?"

Travers nodded weakly. "Think I will," he said.

The time was coming, though, he promised himself as he settled back, when he would get out of here.

And with any luck, it would be before that posse came along.

The only thing was, they should have been here before now. They hadn't been that far behind him, and his tracks should have been easy to follow. Something had to have happened to slow them down or throw them off the trail.

Just how much luck could one man have?

Late that day, Travers felt good enough to try walking again. He made it all the way to the door this time, and although his legs were considerably stronger, he was still glad to have the doorjamb to grab on to.

He opened the door and looked out into the main room. George was nowhere in evidence. The trading post was cluttered with goods, as could be expected. Travers saw saddles and tack, shovels and hoes, barrels of sugar and flour and coffee. There was a counter along one side of the room, and the shelves behind it were loaded with canned peaches.

There was a fine layer of dust over much of the merchandise. It was obvious that George didn't do a whole hell of a lot of business out here.

The big windows in the front of the building were begrimed with years of dust and dirt, but they admitted enough of the late afternoon light for Travers to see as he stepped into the room. There was a sudden flurry of motion to his left, and he spun that way, his hand instinctively going to his hip.

But there was no gun there, of course. Travers let out a yell and ducked as something big and ugly flapped toward him.

The big bird soared over his head and lit on the counter, turning and fixing him with a baleful stare. It was probably the ugliest thing Travers had ever seen, and as he straightened up, he shook his head in disbelief.

This was the first time he had ever seen a buzzard inside a building.

There was a chuckle from the door leading to the porch. "See you met one o' my other patients," George said. He was carrying a bucket of water and had obviously just come from the river.

"What the hell's a buzzard doing in here?"

"Gettin' over what ails it, just like you. Had a busted wing, it did. Couldn't fly worth a darn. Don't know what happened to it, but it'd'a died sure, happen I hadn't helped it out."

"But it's a *buzzard,*" Travers said. "Why would anybody want to help something like that?"

The bird seemed to glare even more at him.

George laughed again. "Reckon there's folks might ask the same sort o' question 'bout you, son. You wasn't just a real purty picture when you showed up at my door."

Travers shrugged and said, "I guess you're right. You take in just any stray that comes along, don't you?"

"Figger somebody's got to." George set the bucket of water on the counter and waved a hand at a pile of clothes stacked there also. "There's your traps. Reckon if you're feelin' better, it wouldn't do no harm to get dressed."

"Thanks." Travers went to the counter and picked up the clothes, moving slowly and carefully. He still had a moment of dizziness every now and then.

When he was dressed, he felt even better. He sat down on a barrel long enough to pull on his boots, then sighed. "Wish I hadn't lost my gun."

George frowned. "You don't need a gun here, son. Ain't no harm goin' to come to you."

"I'm sure it's not, old-timer. But I've been wearing a gun for a long time. Even slept with it a lot of nights. So I don't rightly feel natural without one."

George moved behind the counter and reached into one of the shelves beneath it. He came up with a coiled shell belt and holster and thrust it toward Travers. "Here," he grunted. "If it's that all-fired important to you."

Travers took the weapon and strapped it on, then slipped the Colt out of the holster. He hefted it for balance, checked the loads in the cylinder, did a quick road-agent spin, then slid the pistol back in its sheath. The gun seemed like a good one, and the belt fit him just fine.

"Right good with that noisemaker, ain't you?" George observed dryly.

"I get by," Travers said. He glanced at the window and saw that it was getting dark outside. He would have liked to fire off a few rounds to see how the recoil of the heavy weapon made his wound feel, but that would have to wait until tomorrow. He contented himself with pulling another quick draw.

And as the weight of the gun dragged at his arm, the memory of the clerk's blood splashing on the wall of the express office back at Grady came out of the holster with it.

Travers stopped abruptly, jammed the gun back in the holster. George looked shrewdly at him and said, "Somethin' eatin' on your insides, younker?"

"Yeah," Travers muttered. "Has anybody been by here looking for me?"

"Ain't seed a soul round here for weeks. Why? You got somebody on your trail?"

Travers didn't meet the old man's curious gaze. "Could be. That make a difference to you?"

"Took in a hurt buzzard, didn't I? You reckon it'd make a difference to me?"

Travers grimaced. "There's something I've been trying to tell you for a couple of days now, old man. I think it's time you listened."

"Shoot, if'n you had somethin' on your mind, you should'a spoke up, boy."

Travers wiped the back of a hand across his mouth. "You got anything to drink around here?"

George pushed the bucket of water across the counter toward

him. He said, "Water don't come no better'n this."

Water wasn't what Travers had had in mind, but it looked like that was all he was going to get. Whiskey probably wouldn't be very good for him anyway, not with a hole in his belly.

He took the dipper George handed him and dipped up a long drink of the cold water. Like the old man said, it was good. And it seemed to have the same invigorating effect on Travers that he had experienced when he first stumbled onto Ghost River.

"All right," he said, wiping his mouth again. "I'll just say it plain. I'm an outlaw, George. Me and the boys I ride with were going to hold up the express office over in Grady. I caught that slug in my middle when things went bad."

"Owlhoot, eh?" George didn't seem particularly surprised. "Done a bunch o' thievin', have ye?"

"More than my share. But that's not the worst of it. I . . . I killed a man back there in Grady. Shot him while we were trying to escape."

Putting it in words like that made it suddenly seem even worse to Travers. He didn't know how George would react, but the man would be justified in running him out of here. George probably never would have helped him if he had known Travers was a murderer.

George rubbed his whiskers with a callused palm. "Reckon that there's mighty bad, all right. I knowed somethin' was botherin' you 'sides that bullet hole."

Travers put his palms on the counter and leaned on it, head down. "I never meant to kill him," he said softly. "I just didn't stop to think. The clerk was about to shoot my friend Emory, and I just snapped a shot at him."

"You sure you killed him?"

Travers suddenly realized that he wasn't sure. There had been a lot of blood, and the clerk had gone down like a poleaxed steer, but how could he be sure?

"Does it matter?" Travers asked. "I shot him, I know that. I was trying to kill him."

"You sound mighty sorry 'bout the whole thing now."

"I am," Travers said flatly. "I wish I'd never ridden into Grady with that gang. Hell, I wish I'd never even been born." He thought about his father, about Polly Dawes and her uncle and that big fast horse. "I think everybody would have been a hell of a lot better off."

George stared thoughtfully at him for a long moment, considering everything that Travers had just said. Then he shook his head abruptly. "Ain't no use wishin' that, boy. You was born, and you done all the things you done in your life, and can't nothin' change that. But you can change what happens on down the trail. Nothin' says you got to stay a worthless owlhoot all your life."

Travers looked up and shook his head. "It's no good, George. There'll be a posse showing up here sooner or later, and they'll take me back to prison. If that clerk did die, I'll wind up hanging from a gallows somewhere."

"Reckon you could run. You're 'bout healed up enough to light out again."

Again Travers shook his head. "I'm through running. My life's not worth saving."

The old man bristled. "Here, now. I won't have that kind of talk in my place. Saved that there buzzard, didn't't I?"

"Damned if I know why."

"I'll tell you why, Jacob Travers. That buzzard's got a place in this world, sorry though it may be to a lot of folks. There's a reason for him bein' here. And there's a reason for you, too, even if you ain't found it yet."

Travers's mouth twisted bitterly. "You're starting to sound like a goddamn preacher."

"And you sound like you don't care for bein' preached at."

"My pa was a preacher," Travers said. "And when I got in trouble, he turned his back on me. Quoted scripture at me, then cut me out of his life. The way it all turned out, I reckon he was right to do it, too."

George was silent for a moment, then said, "Just 'cause a man's a preacher don't mean he knows what he's talkin' 'bout. You'd do well to recollect that."

"Like I said, it doesn't matter. That posse's bound to be here soon."

"Well, until they do show up, you keep on gettin' your strength back. You're liable to need it."

"You don't want me to ride on?" Travers was surprised. The old man could get into trouble for helping an outlaw on the dodge.

"You do what you want, boy. But you're welcome to stay, if you've a mind to."

All this standing and talking had worn Travers out. Right now, all he wanted to do was crawl back into that bed and get some more sleep. The old man was right. There was no point in worrying about that posse until they got here.

"Guess I'll stay on a little while longer," Travers said.

"Thought you might."

Travers was undressed and back in bed, the Colt resting on the floor close at hand now, before he suddenly realized that George had called him by name.

He had never told the old man his name. Had he?

He went to sleep wondering about it.

Chapter Five

Travers still hadn't remembered by morning whether he had told George his name or not. He knew that he had been out of his head a lot of the time over the last few days. There was no telling what he had said during those spells.

Hell, it was possible the old man had seen his picture on a wanted poster somewhere and remembered him.

Travers got out of bed and put his pants and boots and gun on, then went into the other room carrying his shirt. He saw George standing behind the counter. Something scurried out of sight around one of the barrels. Travers got enough of a glimpse of the animal to recognize it as a chuckwalla.

The old man seemed to take pity on ugly creatures. The buzzard was perched on a pickle barrel, and now there was a big lizard darting around underfoot. And an outlaw, Travers thought wryly.

"Look like you're feelin' right spry," George said with a toothless grin.

"Feeling good enough to want these bandages off," Travers

told him. "I know it doesn't seem like enough time has passed for that bullet hole to heal, but it sure feels better." He hesitated, then went on, "No sign of that posse yet?"

"Reckon you'd know about it if'n they'd showed up." George came out from behind the counter, carrying a knife. "I don't know 'bout taking them bandages off yet, but if you'll hold still, we'll give 'er a try."

Travers held his breath as the old man sliced through the bandages and unwound them. When George finally grunted to signify that he was through, Travers took a deep breath and waited for the pain of the wound to hit.

There wasn't any.

He tried again, then looked down at his bare torso. There was a big red scar on one side of his stomach, and when he reached around to his back, he could feel a similar mark there. The bullet had gone all the way through, all right, just as he had thought.

But the scars weren't particularly sore, and as he twisted his body from side to side, there were no twinges.

"You best be careful for a few days not to bust it open again," George warned him. "'Pears them old remedies are still the best 'uns. You mended up right nice."

Travers nodded. His progress was a surprise, but he would continue taking any luck he could get.

"Reckon I'll be ready to ride on soon," he said. "I don't want to get you in any trouble, George."

The old man waved off the words. "No need to worry 'bout that none, boy. This here's the onliest tradin' post in this part o' the country. Nobody wants to give ol' George any trouble."

From the looks of things around here, the only trading post or not, George and his business weren't in great demand. Regardless, Travers didn't intend on staying any longer than he had to.

"I'll rest up another day and have me some more of that prairie dog stew of yours," he said. "But then I'll have to be riding."

"Suit yourself." George went to the old wood stove in the corner, where a big pot of the stew always seemed to be simmering. Travers had never seen him actually making the stuff, so he still wasn't sure what was in it. The pot always seemed to be full.

There was coffee on the stove, too. Travers figured it was so good because it was made with the water from Ghost River. He drank several cups of it and put away a couple of bowls of stew, and by the time he was finished he felt more human than he had in days. Better, in fact, than any time he could remember since starting on the outlaw trail.

He stood up from the rough table where he and George had been eating and strolled to the front door of the trading post. The sun hurt his eyes at first when he stepped onto the long porch, but he got used to it quickly and enjoyed the warmth as he settled down on the steps. He had put his shirt back on, and the makings were in his pocket. He rolled a quirly, rasped a lucifer into life, and lit up.

Maybe being alive wasn't so bad after all, he thought.

He heard George's run-down old boots on the planks of the porch behind him, but he didn't turn around. The old man asked, "Been thinkin' 'bout what we said last night?"

"Some," Travers admitted. "I reckon you're right about not being able to change the past. But I'm not sure I can do one damn thing about the future, either."

George snorted. "You're the most argifyin' rascal I ever run across. Why don't you have a little faith in yourself, boy?"

"Never saw much reason to before."

"Well, try it now," the old man said testily. "I'm gettin' a mite tired o' tryin' to convince ya you ain't the worthless skunk you think you are. Dagnab it, there's got to be lots o' things you're good at."

Travers stood up and dropped the cigarette in the sand. He stepped on it, then glanced up at George on the porch. "Sure there is." He gestured with his left hand at a mesquite on the opposite bank of the river. He could see now in the daylight, with the fog gone, that it was about fifty feet across. "See that bush?"

George nodded.

Travers turned square to the river, his gun coming out as he did so. He was firing almost before the barrel leveled, squeezing off five shots so rapidly that the explosions sounded like one long roar.

Every slug cut a branch on the mesquite.

George whistled gustily. "That's mighty fine shootin', son!" he exclaimed.

Travers blinked and stared at the bush. Damned right it was good shooting. He had expected one or two of the bullets to hit the target. He had never dreamed that every single shot would be perfect.

And this Colt had seemed to come out of the holster faster and smoother than the old one had ever done. He was good with a gun and he knew it, better than a lot of men out here, but not as good as he had just demonstrated.

He took fresh cartridges from the shell belt, thumbed the empties out, reloaded. Seating the gun in the holster, he was looking around for another target when George said, "How about these?"

The old man had a handful of crackers from the barrel inside the trading post. Travers shrugged and said, "Sure. Why not?"

Standing on the edge of the porch, George said, "Here goes," and flung the crackers into the air.

Travers palmed the Colt, tipped the barrel up, and fired. Again he emptied the weapon as fast as he could pull the trigger.

Then he stood with his mouth open as a shower of cracker crumbs floated down around him.

"Reckon you're the best man with a gun I ever did see," George said softly.

Something was wrong. Travers knew damn well he couldn't have hit every one of the crackers. But he had seen the evidence with his own eyes. He'd heard all the tales of the fast guns, the shootists and the quick draw artists, the gunslingers. He had never figured to be one of them, though.

Out of habit, he reloaded the Colt, then holstered it. "I don't think I want to shoot anymore," he said.

"Suit yourself." George pointed at a pile of logs stacked against the side of the building. "Since you're feelin' so much better, how 'bout startin' to earn your keep? Them logs come from the hills, but they need splittin' up for firewood."

"Sure." Travers kept the gun on, but he stripped his shirt off again and went over to pick up the ax that was leaning against the side of the building. It had been a long time since he had done any hard physical labor, since before he had left home, in fact. To his surprise, he found himself looking forward to it now.

He went at it slowly, being careful not to put too much strain on his injury. Like George had said, he didn't need to tear the wound open again. But he felt surprisingly strong as he cut the logs into manageable lengths and then split them for firewood. Sweat popped out on him as the sun and the exercise heated him up.

God, it felt good to be alive!

Travers found himself grinning. For all of his preacherlike talk, George had made sense. Travers was sorry for what he had done in the past, but now he wanted to put it behind him, make a new start somewhere.

Knowing it was all a dream made the thoughts bittersweet. The law would catch up to him sooner or later, no matter what he did. He would wind up in jail or hung, and it wouldn't really matter which. Either one would mean death.

But until then, he was going to enjoy the simple things in life, like splitting wood and sweating and prairie dog stew and hot coffee and cold, clear river water.

The ax blade thudded into the wood, and it was a good sound.

Travers worked around the place all day, taking time only to share lunch with George. For the first time, he had a chance to take a good look at the trading post. It was more solid than it appeared at first glance. There was a barn and corral out back where Travers's horse was being kept. Several other fine-looking mounts were there, too, and Travers wondered what the old man needed with horses like that. A cow and a small flock of chickens provided milk and eggs. Travers caught a glimpse of several cats in the barn, but they seemed to be wild and wanted no part of him.

They were probably there to keep the rats and the lizards under control, he thought.

All in all, he realized, this wouldn't be such a bad place to live. George seemed satisfied with it. It had to get lonely at times, however. Travers had been here several days, and no other travelers had passed by in that time. Judging by appearances, they might have been the only two people in five hundred miles.

Travers asked the old man about that over supper that night. "How do you stay in business out here? You can't make any money off pilgrims like me."

"I never set out to get rich, boy," George replied. "If'n money was all I wanted, I'd'a sure done things different. But I figgered it was better to give folks a hand, rather'n stick mine out for what I could get."

"That doesn't answer the question. How do you live?"

"Peaceably, son," George said. "Peaceably."

Travers laughed. Let the old man have his secrets. Maybe he had struck it rich in his prospecting days and didn't need any income now. The more he thought about it, the more likely something along those lines seemed to Travers.

In fact, George could have a fortune stashed out here. Who would ever think it to look at the place? It might not be hard to find, if a man knew how to look—

Travers gave a shake of his head and put those thoughts out of his mind. Back when he was an outlaw—before the gunfight in Grady—he might have considered looting an old man's cache. But not now. And never again, he told himself.

When he glanced up, there was a strangely satisfied look on George's face, just like the old coot knew what he was thinking. Travers growled, "What're you grinning at, mister?"

"Oh, nothin'," George said. "Nothin' at all."

Travers slept well that night, better than he had expected after the long day of work. He had figured that his muscles would be sore and cramped up, but that wasn't the case. When he got out of bed the next morning, there was only a little stiffness.

Travers also knew, as soon as he awoke, that it was time to go. He had to leave Ghost River—today.

He said as much to George, and the old man nodded. "Reckon I knew you'd be gettin' a mite fiddlefooted. Hard for a boy like you to sit still for long, ain't it?"

"That's not it," Travers said. "I want to move on before that posse finds me here."

George snorted. "You been yammerin' 'bout that posse ever since you got here. You ever stop to think maybe they ain't comin' after you?"

"I shot that man—"

"I know you did. But maybe the ones who chased you lost your trail. Been known to happen, you know, even to the best trackers."

Travers considered the idea. George might be right, he decided. It seemed like the pursuit from Grady would have caught up to him by now if it was going to.

He still figured that the law would reach out and put its hand on him sooner or later, but maybe he could postpone that day for a while. Maybe he could accomplish something in the meantime.

"Whether they lost the trail or not, I've still got to go," he said.

"Sure. Didn't mean you shouldn't. There ain't nothin' to keep you here."

"Dammit, George," Travers said, his voice showing his frustration. "You know I appreciate everything you've done for me. Hell, you saved my life! I know that. I'd pay you back if I could."

George faced him with an unexpected fierceness. "You want to pay me back, boy?" he demanded.

Travers nodded, surprised at the old man's vehemence.

"Then forget 'bout bein' an owlhoot," George went on. "You recollect ever'thin' we said the last few days 'bout puttin' the past behind you. You promise me you'll do that?"

"I promise," Travers said.

"Then go on." George waved a hand. "Get your mangy carcass on out'n here."

Travers grinned. "I think you're going to be sorry to see me go, George."

"Don't you believe it! I got better things to do 'n tend to a scraggly, worrisome pup like you!" The old man reached under the counter and brought out a canvas bag and a canteen. "Fixed you up some grub and filled your canteen. Your hoss is saddled up and ready outside."

Frowning, Travers took the bag and the canteen. "You knew, didn't you?"

"Told you I did."

Travers went out onto the porch. As George had said, his horse was ready to go. The animal looked sleek and rested. George had obviously taken good care of it.

Travers hung the bag and the canteen on his saddle, then glanced up at George. The old man stood on the porch, leaning on the railing. "You take care of yourself, old-timer," Travers told him.

"Don't you worry none 'bout me," George assured him. "If'n you ever get back to this part o' the country, I reckon I'll still be right here, waitin'."

"I'll come back and pay you a visit," Travers promised. He swung up into the saddle, met the old man's intense gaze for a moment, then touched the brim of his hat and pulled the horse around.

He rode south.

There was a rise south of the trading post. Travers paused when he reached the crest of it and looked back. George was still standing on the porch, his whiskered face raised to watch Travers. Travers lifted an arm to wave—

And saw, across the river, the group of riders coming toward him.

Even at this distance, he could see sunlight glinting off the badge worn by the man in the lead.

The posse had caught up, all right. It had taken them a long time, but now they were here.

And there was no way they could miss seeing him, skylighted

like he was on the top of the rise. He had been stupid, damned stupid, to come up here just so he could look back over Ghost River. He knew to ride around the high places.

The sound of hoofbeats, a lot of them, came to him through the hot morning air. At any second he expected one of the posse members to spot him and raise a shout. Then the riders would break out their rifles and start shooting at him. He had been chased by posses before; he knew what was going to happen.

Maybe he could outrun them. He started to wheel the horse around and give it the spur. It was a long chance, but the only one he had.

Something stopped him.

As Travers frowned in consternation, the posse began to veer off to the east. From where they were, they couldn't see the river or the trading post yet, and they were acting like they didn't even know the stream was there. Slowly, they swung into a path that paralleled the river.

They either didn't see him—an impossibility at a distance of a quarter of a mile, he thought—or they were ignoring him.

Either way, Travers didn't have the slightest damned idea what to make of it.

But once again, luck had smiled on him, and he wasn't going to spit in its face. The strange paralysis that had seemed to grip him fell away, and he jerked the horse's head around. Glancing down toward the trading post, he saw George waving a farewell at him. Travers swept his hat off, swung it around his head, and slapped the animal's rump with it. He wanted to yell as the horse took off into a ground-eating gallop down the other side of the slope, but he kept his mouth shut. No sense in asking for attention . . . or trouble.

Instead, he kept a broad grin on his face as he raced away from Ghost River.

Chapter Six

For the first few hours, Travers kept an almost constant eye on his back trail. But as the day passed, he gradually came to accept the fact that the posse had somehow missed him. He had expected them to come boiling over the hills behind him at any moment, shooting and hollering.

Around noontime, he stopped to eat some of the food George had packed for him and take a long drink of the cool water in the canteen. As usual, it refreshed him and made the slight ache of the bullet wound in his side go away.

He rode through country that was unfamiliar to him. To the best of his memory, he had never been through these parts before. The terrain was pretty once he left the pine-covered mountains in the distance to the west. As he continued south, he hit another dry stretch, though, the land broken up by an occasional arroyo. There were still enough creeks in the area to keep things from getting too brown, but in country like this, water could sometimes be in short supply.

He was glad he had the canteen. It might be a good idea to make it last as long as he could.

He had been gone from Ghost River for a day and a half before he saw another human being. Then, as he paused on a ridge, he spotted a small jag of cattle being hazed out of a gully by a couple of cowboys. Travers edged his horse over into a stand of brush, for some reason not wanting to be seen. Habit, he decided. He had been on the dodge for too long.

He waited until the cowhands were out of sight, watching the dust raised by the riders and cattle moving off to the east. Then Travers turned his horse's head south again.

Late that afternoon, during one of the periodic halts when he turned in the saddle to look behind him, he saw more dust in the distance. Riders were heading toward him, and from the looks of the dust, they were coming in a hurry. Travers frowned. That wasn't a good sign. On the other hand, there wasn't enough dust for the pursuers to be the posse from Grady.

The sound of gunfire floated through the air to him.

A few minutes later, Travers could hear shouting and the beat of hooves. He wheeled his horse around and put it into an easy run, riding to the crest of a slight hill a hundred yards away. From this spot he could look back and see what was happening.

A wagon being drawn by four horses was bouncing along the rough trail, and three men on horseback were giving chase to it. The wagon was enclosed by wooden walls and a roof, and its sides were painted in gaudy colors.

A medicine-show wagon, Travers decided. He squinted as the wagon flashed by below him, and he tried to make out the ornate writing on the side panels. He couldn't read the words, but he got a good look at the man whipping the team into frenzied speed. He wore a suit and a tall black hat and sported a beard. The person on the bouncing seat beside him drew more of Travers's attention.

A girl, obviously terrified, with long hair the color of midnight being blown by the wind of their flight. . . .

The three men chasing the wagon all had their guns out and were taking occasional shots at the fleeing vehicle. They shouted curses after it. From Travers's vantage point, all three of them looked like cowhands, but this chase smacked of something more than the usual rangeland hoorawing.

This was serious, and at the speed the wagon was making, if it turned over things could get bad in a hurry.

Travers looked over his shoulder. None of the people below had seen him. He could ride down the other side of this slope and be gone within minutes. That was probably the smart thing to do. It didn't pay to mix in other people's business out here.

He sighed heavily. Even not knowing exactly what was going on here, he couldn't turn his back on the situation. Not now.

Travers started his horse down the rise, putting it into a gallop when he reached the relatively flat trail.

Up ahead he saw that the cowboys were gaining on the wagon. As he watched, one of the riders put on a burst of speed and drew even with the team. The man left the saddle in a leap, seeming to fly for an instant as he sailed over the backs of the horses and came down on the off-side leader. It was a trick that could get a man killed very easily, but the cowboy pulled it off to perfection. He hauled back on the lines, bringing the team to an unwilling halt.

The other two raced up to the wagon and threw themselves down from their saddles. They ran to the seat. The driver tried to put up a fight, but one of the men grabbed his coat and yanked him off the wagon. A hard fist sent him sprawling.

The girl let out a scream as the other man caught hold of her and pulled her off the wagon. She struggled, but her strength was no match for the cowboy. He had a grin on his face, Travers saw as he rode closer.

It looked like the sides were choosing themselves for him.

The man wrestling with the girl slapped her, the crack of the blow splitting the air. He shoved her, and she sat down hard on the ground as her balance deserted her. She slumped there, sobbing, as the man stood over her.

On the other side of the wagon, the driver had lost his tall hat as he was pounded by his captor.

None of them seemed to be paying any attention to Travers. He yanked his horse to a stop a few yards away, and finally someone noticed him. The cowboy who had made the daring leap onto the wagon team looked up and saw him. "Coley!" he yelped.

The man who was beating up the driver of the wagon stopped with his fist raised for another blow. His head jerked around in the direction indicated by the one who had cried out.

Travers sat his horse calmly, his hands resting on the saddlehorn. He said, "You'd better have a good reason for treating those folks like that, mister."

The man called Coley stared at him. Dark shaggy hair and a thick mustache gave him a fierce look, but Travers met his glare without flinching. After a moment, Coley rumbled, "My reasons ain't none of your damn business, hombre."

As if to prove his point, he started his fist toward the bloody face of the man he was holding up with his other hand.

Travers drew his Colt and fired in one smooth motion, the bullet smacking past Coley's head. It was a deliberate miss, but it came close enough to make the man yell and turn loose his victim. As the bearded man slumped against the wagon and then fell to the ground, Coley started to turn toward Travers. His hand went to the gun on his hip.

Travers pulled back the hammer of his gun, not hurrying. "Don't," he said simply.

Coley stopped his motion. His face contorted with frustration and fury as he regarded Travers. "I told you," he said in a low voice that trembled with rage, "my reasons ain't none of your business."

"I'm making them my business. Now tell me what's going on here."

Coley waved a big hand at the bearded man, who was drawing in ragged breaths through his bloodied nose and mouth. "I'm dealin' out justice," Coley snapped. "This man's a murderer."

That threw Travers for a moment. He frowned. "You a lawman?"

Coley shook his head. "No, but that don't change things none. This son of a bitch killed my nephew!"

Wearily, the bearded man shook his head in denial of the charge. From the other side of the wagon, the girl cried out, "That's not true!"

Travers had been keeping an eye on the girl and the other man as best he could. From where he sat, he could see all of the little group clustered around the wagon, but it wasn't easy. He was waiting for the man who had been molesting the girl to make some sort of move. Now the girl came hurrying around the back of the wagon and dropped to her knees beside the bearded man. She cradled his head in her lap.

The young man who was still seated on one of the team's leaders said mockingly, "Now ain't that a touchin' sight!"

Travers saw that this one was young, little more than a kid really, with curly blond hair and a mouth that twisted into a natural sneer. Probably he was only a few years younger than Travers himself, but there was a softness about his face that said he hadn't been down nearly as many trails.

Glancing at the wagon itself, Travers saw that his initial impression had been right. The fancy curlicue letters proclaimed it to be the wagon of Dr. Milburn Pritchard, purveyor of the world-famous Isom's Elixir. Travers had never heard of Isom's Elixir, but he imagined it was more of the same snake oil that was hawked all over the West. The bearded man had to be Dr. Pritchard, and even though Travers had not heard his spiel, he knew that the so-called doctor would claim the elixir cured all manner of ills. The girl probably did a little song-and-dance act to lure the suckers in the first place.

She was pretty, Travers saw now, as pretty as you would expect such a girl to be. Her long hair shone in the sun, and her features were beautiful, even twisted with worry as they were at the moment. The simple cotton dress she wore did little to conceal the curves of her slender body.

As she said anxiously, "Are you all right, Dr. Pritchard?" Travers noticed that there was a strange accent in her voice. He had heard folks from England a time or two in his life, and he decided that was where she was from.

All of which didn't matter a damn right now, not when he had a gun in his hand and three angry men in front of him.

"Look, just tell me what it's all about," he suggested reasonably to Coley.

"I told you. This here quack doctor killed my nephew with his goddamn elixir! My brothers and I come after him to settle the score."

Pritchard struggled to a sitting position, ignoring the girl's efforts to make him lie back. A fresh trickle of blood ran down from his mouth into his neatly trimmed salt-and-pepper beard as he exclaimed, "That's a bloody lie! I had nothing to do with that lad's death."

Coley glared at him. "The boy was sick and you give him your tonic. He was dead an hour later!" he roared.

"His appendix burst!" Pritchard shot back. He was obviously still very frightened, but he was not going to let Coley's accusations go unanswered. "If I had been given the opportunity to examine him, I might have been able to diagnose his illness. Your other brother merely said that his boy had an upset stomach. I thought Isom's Elixir was just the thing to get him back on his feet."

The young man on the horse snapped, "Instead it got poor Jamie in a hole in the ground, you bastard!"

Travers had been listening to the argument with mixed emotions. He had never had any dealings with medicine show men; he'd preferred to waste his money in other ways. But he knew the reputation most of them had. The tonics they peddled did more harm than good most of the time, although there were always people who swore by the remedies. It was all too possible that the stuff sold by Pritchard had indeed hurt the nephew of these men.

But if what Pritchard said was right, there had been an honest misunderstanding involved. It didn't seem right to hold Pritchard responsible if he had never even seen the sick boy.

Travers grimaced. When he had ridden down here, he hadn't counted on sticking his nose into something this complicated. His life had been pretty simple up to this point—take what you need and always watch your back. He was an outlaw—had been an outlaw, he corrected himself, until stumbling on to Ghost River—not some damn lawyer. But he had dealt himself this hand, and now he had to play it.

"If you've got a complaint against these folks, you take it to the law," he told Coley. "You're not going to rough them up or kill them on your own."

"We handle our own problems where we come from, mister," Coley replied. "And we can hang two as easy as one."

"What about the girl?"

For the first time, the third man spoke. He was the one who had been wrestling with the girl, and the grin on his face said that he had come along for more than justice. "We'll settle the score with her our own way, too, mister."

Travers saw the man tense and knew he was about to try something. He started to twist that way, and he saw that he couldn't cover all three of them. The third man suddenly ducked behind the wagon.

Coley grabbed for his gun as Travers went out of the saddle in a dive. The only thing that saved Travers was that Pritchard suddenly lurched forward, banging into Coley and knocking him off balance. Coley's shot kicked up dust a couple of yards to the side as Travers landed hard on the ground.

The Colt was still in Travers's hand when he landed, and he triggered off a shot. The bullet thudded into Coley's chest and drove him backward into the team of horses. Scared by the gunfire, the animals danced nervously in their harness, and the young man sitting on one of them was dumped unceremoniously under their hooves. He let out a yell and scrambled for safety.

The third man came running back out from behind the wagon, the pistol in his hand spitting flame. Travers rolled as the slugs knocked grit into his eyes. Blinking, he aimed as much by sound as anything else and let go with two more shots. His vision cleared in time to see the third man knocked spinning by the bullets.

Travers came up on his knees and swung toward the last of the men, the young one. The boy had managed to get out from under the team without getting trampled, but he had dropped his gun in the process. He was bending over and reaching for it when Travers barked, "Hold it!"

Slowly, Travers got to his feet. He kept the gun trained on the young man. The girl was sitting on the ground crying, and Pritchard was standing and looked stunned by the violence.

Quickly Travers checked Coley and the other man. He was ready to put more lead into them if they moved, but both of them were dead, he discovered.

Three dead now. These two and the clerk back in Grady. He was getting good at this.

The bitter thought flashed through Travers's head, but he couldn't feel too guilty about what had happened here. Coley and the other one had been shooting at him, after all, and if he hadn't interfered in the first place, there was no doubt they would have hung Pritchard and assaulted the girl. They had admitted as much.

"Kick that gun over here," Travers told the young man.

The boy did as he was ordered. There were tears in his eyes as he stared at the bodies of his brothers, but he kept his hands half lifted and didn't try anything.

Travers picked up the young man's pistol and tucked it behind his belt. Without taking his eyes off the boy, he said, "Dr. Pritchard?"

"Y-Yes?" The doctor sounded shaken.

"Can you round up the horses these men were riding?"

"I–I believe so."

The girl sniffed and brought her crying under control. She got unsteadily to her feet. "I'll . . . I'll help you, Doctor," she said.

While Travers kept the young man covered, Pritchard and the girl caught the horses and brought them over to the wagon. Travers said, "Tie them onto the back of the wagon."

The young man overcame his grief and fear long enough to say angrily, "You can't steal our horses!"

"I'm not stealing them, boy," Travers told him. "You'll find them about a mile on down the trail. That way you can take your brothers back where you came from."

"Or I could come after you!"

Travers shook his head. "I wish you wouldn't. I don't like killing folks."

"All right," Pritchard said. "We have the horses secured." He bent over to pick up his hat from where it had fallen in the dust. He brushed it off and settled it back on his head.

Travers gestured with the barrel of his Colt. "Move away from the wagon," he told the young man.

Grudgingly, the young man moved. The look on his face made it plain that he wanted to put up a fight, but he knew that doing so would mean death.

With practiced ease, Travers mounted his own horse while still holding the gun. Pritchard and the girl climbed onto the seat of the wagon. Bending far forward, Pritchard managed to catch hold of the lines he had dropped earlier. "We can commence now," he told Travers. "I assume you will be accompanying us, sir?"

"For a while," Travers replied. Now that he had butted into this mess, he didn't feel like he could abandon the two little lambs he had rescued. He looked intently at the young man and asked, "What's your name?"

For a moment he looked as if he was going to stubbornly refuse to answer. Then he finally said, "Sorenson. Dale Sorenson. Those were my brothers Coley and Bramwell you just killed, mister." His voice broke slightly on the last sentence.

"Well, I'm sorry, Dale," Travers said. "I really am. But your brothers started the shooting. As bad as this is, why don't you let it be the end of it? Things don't have to get worse."

Dale Sorenson shook his head. "No, mister, I'll find you again. I've got more brothers, and you won't be able to hide from us forever. You want this to end here, you'll have to gun me down right now."

Travers sighed heavily. "There was a time I might've done that, boy. You just think on what I told you. And I *am* sorry."

He waved his free hand at the wagon. "Come on, Doc, get 'em rolling."

Travers kept his gun drawn until they were out of sight of Dale Sorenson. He watched the boy's dwindling figure over his shoulder. Sorenson stood alone, next to the bodies of his brothers, his face turned toward Travers and the wagon.

Travers had a hunch he would be seeing Dale Sorenson again, and he didn't like the feeling at all.

When they had gone a mile, Travers motioned for Pritchard to stop the wagon. He rode to the back, leaned over, and untied the reins of the trailing horses. Then he moved up next to the wagon seat and said, "We'll have a good enough lead by the time that boy hoofs it up here that he won't be able to catch up. Anyway, after he finds these horses, I think he'll go back to collect his brothers and take them home."

Pritchard smiled unsteadily up at him. "I'm sure I don't know how to convey my appreciation to you, sir. Without your assistance, those ruffians would have surely killed us."

"They'd have had a necktie party, all right." Travers jerked his head. "You'd better get moving again. We can talk while we're riding."

When the wagon was rolling again, Pritchard stuck out a hand to Travers and said, "Dr. Milburn Pritchard, at your service, sir."

Travers shook his hand and nodded toward the side of the wagon. "So I see."

"And this charming young lady beside me is my assistant, Miss Leanne Covington."

Travers touched the brim of his hat. "Pleased to meet you, ma'am," he said coolly.

The girl murmured something and didn't look up at him, and that was all right with Travers. She was beautiful, all right, and maybe as charming as Pritchard made her out to be, but ever since Polly Dawes had pulled her little trick with Colonel Jeb Stuart, Travers had tried to steer clear of females as much as possible.

"I assure you, the charges being leveled against me by that horrible man were all completely untrue," Pritchard was saying.

"Did the boy die like he said?" Travers asked.

Pritchard shrugged. He lifted a hand to wipe sweat off his forehead. "I suppose so. But as I told the man, I thought I was dealing with a simple upset stomach. There was no way I could know without examining the boy that his appendix had ruptured."

"I don't know much about medicine, except for patching up bullet holes, but it sounds to me like you're not really to blame, Doc." Travers frowned. "That doesn't mean I'm sold on that so-called elixir of yours."

"Ah, you've heard all the terrible stories about the medicine shows and the snake-oil peddlers! I can tell a skeptic when I see one, my boy." Pritchard was obviously recovering somewhat from the harrowing experience they had gone through. "By the way, I don't believe you told us your name."

"Travers," he said shortly.

"Well, Mr. Travers, I don't blame you a bit for doubting the veracity of my claims when I discourse on the wonderful efficacy of Isom's Elixir. Why, any reasonable man might perhaps balk when first acquainted with the almost unbelievable potency of this miracle concoction—"

The girl let out a moan and slumped against the side of the seat. She started crying again.

Travers had to suppress a grin as Pritchard said, "Ah . . . perhaps Leanne wearies of hearing my enthusiasm for my product. As my assistant, she of course is at my side when I offer these good frontier folk the opportunity to purchase our revitalizing tonic."

"Save the sales pitch," Travers told him. "Just where did this happen with the boy who died?"

"Back up the trail forty or fifty miles. A small community called Dempsey. The Sorenson family owns a ranch near there, I believe. Rather a large clan of them, from what I hear."

Travers was afraid of that. Dale Sorenson had claimed he would resume the chase with some of his other brothers. There was a good chance Travers had bought into something that could prove long and bloody.

As always, though, he had made up his own mind, and now he would have to live with that decision. "Where are you folks headed?"

"We were on our way to a town called La Junta. Would you happen to be familiar with it, Mr. Travers?"

Travers had heard of the place. "Cattle town, isn't it?"

"Yes, indeed. My son owns a 'spread,' I believe he calls it, near there."

Travers frowned in puzzlement. If Pritchard's son owned a ranch, what was the man doing gallivanting around the territory in a medicine-show wagon?

And he was traveling with a young girl who was obviously not a relative of his, either. That was pretty scandalous in itself. Not that anybody else's personal life was any of his business, Travers reminded himself.

It was probably a good thing Pritchard was headed for his son's ranch. Travers could ride along until they got there, and then once the doctor and the girl were among friends, he wouldn't feel bad about riding on and leaving them.

Let Pritchard's family deal with the Sorensons, he decided. He didn't want any part of a feud.

"You haven't said where you were bound for before you so gallantly intervened in our dilemma, Mr. Travers," Pritchard said.

Travers had to think about that one for a minute. "Anywhere else besides where I am, Doc," he finally said. "That's where I'm bound.

Chapter Seven

They stopped to camp that night in a little valley where a small, spring-fed creek bubbled to the top of the ground. It was a pretty place, with plenty of graze for the horses, but Travers was too nervous to appreciate it. If he had been alone, he would have pushed on through the night, just to put some more distance between himself and Dale Sorenson.

Pritchard couldn't drive the wagon in the dark, though, and anyway the team was worn out from its mad dash earlier in the day.

Travers unsaddled his horse and then helped Pritchard unhitch the team. The animals were grateful for the chance to sample the grass, which had not yet turned brown with the summer heat.

When they were done with the team, Pritchard took a bucket from the back of the wagon and thrust it toward Leanne Covington. "Here you are, my dear," he said. "Fetch us some water like a good girl, eh?"

While his words were friendly enough on the surface, Travers could hear the tone of command in the man's voice. Pritchard was obviously accustomed to giving the girl orders.

"We'd better make a cold camp," Travers said. "Just in case anybody's following us, no sense in telling them where we are with a fire."

"Oh, dear, and I was so looking forward to a hot cup of tea." Pritchard shrugged. "Ah, well, one must make certain sacrifices in life, mustn't one?"

That was true enough, Travers supposed, but he made no reply to the Englishman's comment. He had learned during the afternoon that both Pritchard and Leanne hailed from London and that they had been in this country for only a couple of years, even though Pritchard's son, Galen, had made the crossing more than a decade earlier. Pritchard had provided the information in an almost nonstop monologue.

The girl had said very little—next to nothing in fact. And she still wouldn't look at Travers.

That was fine with him.

It would be better all around if Leanne continued to ignore him.

She fetched the water, just as Pritchard told her, and brought jerky and cold biscuits from the wagon. Judging from Pritchard's expression as the early evening shadows gathered over the camp, he was less than pleased with the supper. Travers thought the meal was fine; he'd made do with a lot less plenty of times in his life.

The water from the creek was good, but not as good as that from Ghost River. Travers felt a little guilty for not sharing what was left in his canteen. Not guilty enough to do anything about it, though.

When they were done with their meal, he leaned his back against the trunk of a small tree and stretched his legs out in front of him. For the moment he felt pretty good. He wondered what old George was doing back at the trading post. Probably nursing some other hapless critter he had taken in, Travers thought with a slight grin.

Moonlight made the wagon throw deep shadows. Pritchard was

sitting next to one of the wheels, and Leanne was a few feet away from him. Travers could barely make out both of them.

"Well, my boy," Pritchard said, "I assume that if we are not permitted to have a campfire that lighting a cigar would also be an unwise move."

"I think so," Travers nodded. "You'd be surprised how far away somebody can spot a lucifer being struck."

"You impress me as a man who knows what he is talking about, sir, so I shall bow to your superior knowledge."

"I've ridden down a trail or two," Travers admitted with a smile.

"Would it be a breach of frontier etiquette to inquire as to your past, Mr. Travers?"

For a moment Travers stiffened in instinctive reaction to the question. But then he made himself relax. Pritchard didn't mean any harm.

"Talk like that'd get you shot some places," he answered dryly. "I don't mind telling you, though. I come from a little town a good ways north of here, but I haven't been there in a couple of years. I left home to ride the trails."

"Ah, to see the elephant, as I believe the phrase goes."

"Yeah, I guess you could say that. But it was more of a matter of not wanting to see the inside of a jail."

Pritchard leaned forward. "You're an outlaw?"

"I didn't start out to be," Travers shrugged. "Some folks said I tried to steal a horse, but that's not the way it was. I didn't wait around for the trial, because I knew how it was going to turn out."

He had always been careful before not to talk too much about his past. You never knew when things could catch up to you. For some reason he didn't feel the need for that caution now. Maybe the experience he had been through had changed his way of looking at things. Maybe he was willing to trust people a little more. He just hoped that trust wouldn't wind up getting him killed.

"I've been drifting ever since I took off from that jail," he went on. "Reckon I did some things I'm ashamed of now, but it seemed like the trail to follow at the time."

"You're very good with your gun," Pritchard commented. "I would imagine that there is no shortage of work for a man of your talents."

"I never sold my gun," Travers replied quietly. "I've known men who did, but that was never my line."

For the first time in hours, Leanne spoke up. "But those men today weren't the first you've killed, were they?"

"Leanne!" Pritchard exclaimed before Travers could answer her question. "That's not the type of thing you ask a man, my dear."

Travers shook his head. "I don't mind. No, Miss Covington, those weren't the first . . . I don't think. I may have killed one man before, but I'm not sure. I was in a hurry at the time."

"Escaping from some other bothersome situation?" she said, disapproval evident in her voice.

"Trying to keep from getting killed," he shot back. That wasn't strictly true, since the clerk back in Grady hadn't been threatening *him,* but explaining about Emory Moore was too complicated, Travers decided.

"I'm afraid Leanne is not too fond of some of your western customs, Mr. Travers," Pritchard said. "She, ah, considers most of you barbarians." His voice took on a harsh tone as he continued, "Rather presumptuous of her to pass judgment on others, I believe, considering her own background."

Travers wasn't sure what to make of them. There was obviously some hostility between them, fostered no doubt by Pritchard's commanding attitude. Yet Travers couldn't bring himself to actually dislike the man.

Luckily he thought, he wouldn't have to worry about it for long. In a day or so they would be in La Junta, and Travers could leave them at the ranch owned by Pritchard's son. He could push on south then, maybe cross the border into Mexico. He'd never been there.

Leanne made no reply to Pritchard's gibe. She stood up and

went to the back of the wagon, opening the little door there and disappearing inside. She probably had a bunk in there, Travers thought.

He was about ready to get some sleep himself. He had considered standing watch tonight in case anyone was coming after them, but he trusted his horse to warn him if strangers came too close. The animal was good about that. Anyway, he had plenty of experience at sleeping with one eye and ear open. Being on the dodge taught that to a man.

Travers spread his blankets near the tree and positioned his saddle to use for a pillow. He didn't know what Pritchard intended to do, but he was still surprised when the man stood up, stretched, and said, "Well, good night, sir." The Englishman went to the wagon and entered it.

Travers frowned. He was no prude—nobody who'd been in what seemed like half the whorehouses west of the Mississippi could be—but the scandalous nature of the arrangement still bothered him. It could be that there was absolutely nothing going on between Pritchard and Leanne, but it still looked mighty bad for them to be sharing the wagon.

As he stretched out and rolled up in the blankets, the sounds that began to come from the wagon removed any doubt of what was occurring inside. Travers grimaced and shook his head. He tilted his hat down over his eyes and tried to go to sleep.

None of his business, he told himself. None of his damned business at all.

The night was quiet, and Travers was up long before either of the other two. He had a small fire going and coffee boiling when Pritchard stuck his head out the back of the wagon.

"Good morning!" the Englishman said heartily. "I see you decided to make a fire after all."

Travers glanced up at the sky, gray with dawn. "Smoke's not too noticeable this time of morning, and it's already too light for the fire itself to be seen very far. Safe enough, I'd say. Besides, it's harder to make do with a cold breakfast than a cold supper."

"Indeed." Pritchard stepped down from the wagon and moved over by the fire. He was wearing his vest and tie but no coat. "No trouble during the night, eh? Slept well, did you, my friend?"

"Well enough," Travers grunted. "I reckon that Sorenson boy went on back home like I told him to."

"Yes, but will he take up his ill-advised quest once more when he gets there? That is the question, Mr. Travers."

"He seemed like the kind who doesn't give up easily," Travers said. He took the coffee off the fire and replaced it with a small skillet full of bacon, the last of the provisions that George had sent with him from Ghost River.

"Well, with you accompanying us, I doubt that we have very much to fear from the lad." Pritchard picked up a tin cup and carefully filled it with coffee from the pot.

Travers didn't reply. Pritchard obviously thought that he was going to ride along with them, maybe even stay with them once they reached La Junta. Travers didn't want to take the trouble to disabuse him of that notion right at the moment. There would be time enough for that later.

Leanne Covington came out of the wagon. Travers glanced up at her. He had to admit she was a beautiful woman, even this early in the morning. And that was downright rare. She was wearing the same plain, dark blue dress she had worn the day before, and her black hair was pulled back away from her face and tied in a loose knot.

Her eyes met his, and he quickly looked away. She was Pritchard's woman, pure and simple, and he didn't want either one of them thinking he was interested in her. Trouble of that sort he could do without.

As she knelt beside the so-called doctor, though, and filled her own coffee cup, they struck Travers as a pretty mismatched pair. Pritchard was at least fifty, probably more, while the girl seemed to be in her early twenties. His face, while still handsome, was lined and somewhat leathery, and years of dissipation showed in the pouches underneath his eyes. There was something about

Leanne that still smacked of freshness, even innocence, despite what Travers had heard going on in the wagon the night before.

That freshness was fading in the girl. Before too many more years passed, the life she was living would have stolen the last of her youth, leaving her as jaded as Pritchard.

The Englishman drank half his coffee with a shudder, then pulled a bottle of dark glass from his coat pocket. Travers saw that the label proclaimed it to be Isom's Elixir as Pritchard tipped some of the contents into his coffee cup.

"I see you believe in what you're selling," Travers said dryly.

Pritchard sipped the mixture and then licked his lips. "Naturally. A physician has to believe in what he prescribes. As they say out here in this magnificent wilderness, it's good for what ails you."

Travers took the bacon off the fire. "Are you really a doctor?"

Pritchard frowned, and for a moment Travers thought he was going to lose his temper. But then Pritchard smiled and said, "Again I must deal with the unsavory reputation which others far less scrupulous than I have accrued to my profession. Yes, dear boy, I am a doctor. I was educated at the finest schools in England and gave up a thriving practice to make the voyage to your shining shores. I missed my son, Galen, you see, and when he wrote and asked me to come, I could not refuse him." Pritchard's smile widened. "If I was not a medical man, would I have named my only offspring after the first and greatest of physicians?"

"Reckon not," Travers grunted. He had gotten more of an answer than he had expected. Bluntly, he asked, "What about your wife?"

Pritchard shook his head. "Dead these many years, alas. Her passing was one reason Galen decided to seek his fortune in the New World."

The New World. Travers had never heard the expression before, but it made sense that folks in England, far away across the ocean, would regard his country as just that. To him, though, it was the only world he had ever known, the only one he likely ever would.

"Reason I asked about you being a doctor is that I picked up a bullet in a little fracas awhile back," he said. "It's pretty well healed up, but I thought if it started giving me trouble, you could look at it." He might be asking for trouble, he knew, because despite his claims Pritchard might just be the biggest quack to ever walk the face of the earth. Travers knew enough about bullet holes not to be led too far wrong, however.

"Why, certainly. I'd be glad to check your wound anytime. Who took care of it for you, one of your local practitioners?"

Travers grinned. "Nope. An old man who runs a trading post north of here slapped some kind of secret remedy on it and fed me prairie dog stew until I got my strength back. It seemed to do the trick."

Pritchard wagged a finger at him as he chewed a mouthful of the bacon. "You can't be too careful, my boy, especially when it comes to medicine. I'll perform a quick examination for you after breakfast."

Travers thought the offer over and nodded. It wouldn't hurt anything for Pritchard to just look at the wound. He sure as hell wasn't going to drink any of that elixir, though. There was no telling what was in it other than alcohol, and he could get plenty of that in a whiskey bottle when they got to La Junta.

When the meal was over, Pritchard said carelessly to Leanne, "Clean those things up, won't you, darling?" She moved to take the pan and the coffeepot from Travers, who had been preparing to clean them himself in the sand of the creek. She said nothing as she went about the work.

Pritchard gestured for Travers to follow him, and the two men went around to the other side of the wagon.

"Step into my examining room," Pritchard said with a smile. "If you'll kindly remove your shirt, I'll just have a look-see at that wound."

Travers stripped off the shirt. George had not only cleaned the bloodstains out of it, the old man had mended the bullet tears, too. The patched places were visible on the front and back of the shirt.

"Well, let's take a look," Pritchard muttered as he stooped

slightly to examine the scars. He suddenly straightened, the muscles of his face strangely taut. He rapped, "Turn around."

Travers turned, frowning as he did so. "What's the matter, Doc? The holes aren't festering up, are they?" Actually, the wound felt even better today. Without the scars, Travers wouldn't have known the bullet had ever hit him.

"No, there's no sign of infection," Pritchard said slowly. "I take it the bullet went all the way through."

"Sure did. In the front and out the back. Took a lot of blood with it."

"Yes. Ah . . . everything looks fine, my boy. I'd say you don't have a thing to worry about."

Travers shrugged back into the shirt. "Well, that's good to know. I reckon old George did a good job."

"Yes, indeed. A well-nigh miraculous job, I'd venture to say. . . ." Pritchard went back around the wagon muttering to himself as Travers tucked his shirt in.

The Englishman had sure looked funny when he saw the scars, Travers thought, but that was probably because he didn't want to admit that an old geezer like George had done just as good a job of patching them up as a regular doctor could have. He went back around the wagon and found Leanne giving water to the horses. Pritchard had vanished into the wagon.

Travers went over to the girl and reached out to take the bucket from her. "Let me help you," he said.

"I can do it." She held on to the bucket and carried it over to Travers's horse. "I'm used to tending to such chores."

"Yeah, but you don't have to while I'm traveling with you."

"I said I'd do it," she snapped.

Travers backed off, holding his hands up in mock surrender. "All right," he said. If the girl didn't want his help, he wasn't going to force it on her.

Pritchard came out of the wagon wearing his swallowtail coat and top hat. He rubbed his hands together enthusiastically. "Well, shall we get under way?" he asked. Evidently he had forgotten about whatever was bothering him before.

"Sounds good to me," Travers said. He bent to pick up his saddle and headed toward his horse.

Within fifteen minutes, they had the team hitched up and the wagon rolling. Travers rode alongside for the most part, occasionally scouting ahead a quarter mile or so. He also kept a close watch on their back trail, but there was no sign of trouble in front or behind.

The morning passed pleasantly enough. When they stopped at noontime, Leanne cooked beans and biscuits for their meal. The girl was too quiet and none too friendly, Travers thought, but she was a fair hand when it came to grub.

As usual, Pritchard was talkative. He started with his shipboard journey from England to New York and enlightened Travers on what must have been every trivial detail of his life since then. Travers noticed that he glossed over his relationship with Leanne, however. Pritchard mentioned that she had worked for him in London and had decided to come along with him when he set out for the States, but other than that he said little about her. And she certainly didn't volunteer any information about herself. She was just about the most closemouthed female Travers had ever seen.

Pritchard didn't press him for any more stories about being an owlhoot, and Travers was grateful for that. He studied the country through which they were riding, trying to remember the rough maps he had seen and the tales he had heard. If his memory was right, they would probably reach La Junta sometime the next morning. They could have made it to the cattle town that night, he decided, if they were to push on once darkness fell.

That was too chancy. Pritchard handled the wagon well, but Travers didn't trust him to drive it over an unfamiliar trail at night.

Late that afternoon, while Travers was riding about fifty yards in front of the wagon, he topped a small hill and reined in to study the little valley on the other side. A flicker of brightly colored motion caught his eye.

He tensed, his hand ready to go to his gun, until he realized that the group of men clustered in a clearing below weren't paying any attention to him. They were too busy lifting another man into his saddle on the back of a nervous horse. The man had his hands lashed behind his back.

Travers turned and looked at the wagon. Pritchard had it moving along at a good clip. It would be topping the hill in another couple of minutes. Travers glanced again at the scene in the clearing.

The men had forced their captive's horse to prance over underneath a good-sized tree. Travers licked his lips and abruptly noticed how dry they were as he saw the end of a rope being tossed over a limb of the tree.

He held up a hand to stop the wagon. It wouldn't be a good idea for Pritchard to go blundering into what was about to happen.

"What's wrong, Mr. Travers?" Pritchard asked as he brought the team to a stop just below the top of the hill.

Travers jerked his head toward the valley on the other side. "Going to be a hanging," he said flatly.

Chapter Eight

"A hanging?" Pritchard was aghast. He stood up on the seat of the wagon and peered past Travers, trying to see over the top of the rise. "You can't be serious."

Travers glanced at Leanne Covington and saw that the girl had gone pale under the tan she had acquired from the time spent riding the medicine wagon. He said, "I'm serious, all right. And I think we'd best wait right here until it's all over."

Leanne's breath was coming faster now. Her face was set in tight lines that showed the strain she was feeling. Before Travers knew what she was doing, she leaped down from the wagon seat and ran to the crest of the hill. As she took in the details of the potentially grisly scene below, she put a hand to her breast and swayed slightly.

Travers dropped out of the saddle, thinking she was going to faint, but she had steadied herself by the time he reached her side. He put out a hand anyway and rested it on her arm.

She turned an icy gaze on him. "Are you going to just stand here and let them murder that man?" she asked.

From the wagon, Pritchard put in, "I must agree, Mr. Travers.

We have to do something to stop this heinous crime."

Travers took a deep breath. They probably wouldn't understand, but he had to try to explain. "We don't know those men down there, and it's not a good idea to go messing with folks you don't know," he said. "We don't know what the fella did to get hung, either."

Despite his words, he felt a nagging itch in his own conscience. He knew from bitter experience how easy it was for a man to be accused of something he didn't do. Once the lynch fever hit a bunch of men, there was no reasoning with them. An innocent man could talk himself blue in the face, and the mob still wouldn't believe him.

He realized he was still holding Leanne's arm when she jerked it angrily out of his grip. "You won't put a stop to it?" she demanded.

"Well, ma'am, I don't see how—"

"Then I'll have to!"

Travers watched her for a second before realizing that she intended to march right down the hill into the thick of the riders. He took a quick step and grabbed her arm, pulling her back. "All right," he said with a grimace. "No promises, but I'll see what I can do."

"And I shall accompany you, sir," Pritchard said. He sat down and took up the reins again.

Travers turned toward him. "You'll do no such thing," he said firmly. "You and Miss Covington are staying right up here where you'll be safe. Either that, or I ride away and you're on your own."

"Oh, all right, very well," Pritchard snapped. "Just get down there and stop those vigilantes."

Travers gave a disgusted shake of his head and started the horse down the hill. He didn't know who he was disgusted with, the two from England or himself for going along with their wishes. And if he didn't hurry, it wouldn't matter.

From the looks of things, the prisoner was going to be dancing on air in about another ten seconds.

Several men on the outside of the circle of riders heard him coming and craned their heads around to see who the newcomer was. Travers saw them speaking to other men in the group, and within seconds their attention had shifted from the tied-up man to him. It wasn't too comfortable a feeling.

Travers rode to within twenty feet of the group and reined in. Setting easy in his saddle, he nodded and said, "Howdy, gents. Having some trouble here?" He was a lot more tense than he looked or sounded. The men were staring at him with plenty of curiosity and more than a little anger. They had to be wondering who he was to interrupt their party.

There was no reply from any of the men for a moment. Then, as if in answer to some unspoken command, several of them pulled their horses to the side to create an opening in the circle. Another man rode slowly through the gap to face Travers.

"This here's a private matter, mister," the man said heavily as he stopped, facing Travers. "If you're offerin' to help, we appreciate it. But we can handle things ourselves. Thanks anyway."

"I've never helped string a man up, at least not yet," Travers told him. "Mind telling me what he did?"

The spokesman for the group stared intently at Travers with eyes narrowed from long years of exposure to the elements.

"Don't see as it's any of your business, son," he said, "but since you asked, he's a goddamn rustler, that's what."

Maybe sensing that he had only a slim chance of avoiding death, the prisoner twisted his head around and turned a terrified face toward Travers. "It's a lie, mister!" he said shakily. "I never stole no cattle, not never!"

Travers glanced at the man, not wanting to take his attention off the group's leader for long. He saw a thin, dark-haired puncher with a lantern jaw and wide, scared eyes. The prisoner wasn't a very impressive specimen, but that didn't make him a rustler.

Looking back at the group's leader—who was more than likely the owner of whatever spread they happened to be on—Travers said, "You got proof he stole your cattle?"

"This is my range," the man snapped, confirming Travers's guess. "The only proof I need is my word."

Travers's hands were resting on his saddlehorn. He leaned forward and glanced over his shoulder. Pritchard and the girl were staying out of sight, so he had that much to be thankful for. He didn't much like the looks that he was getting from the riders scattered around the clearing. They didn't care for the interruption of what they considered justice.

Stalling for time while he tried to figure out what to do, Travers looked at the leader and said, "No offense, but who would you be, mister?"

"Name's Forrest Buckston, if it's any of your business. My friends call me Buck. Reckon you can call me Mr. Buckston. And I don't care if it offends you or not, but who the hell are *you*?"

Travers swallowed. He wondered if word of the would-be robbery at Grady had gotten this far, and if it had, had he been identified? That wasn't very likely, he decided, and he had never been one for using a phony name like some did.

"I'm Jacob Travers," he said. "Rode in from up north a ways. I'm not in the habit of mixing in things that are none of my business, Mr. Buckston, but I don't like to see a man being hanged, either."

One of the other men laughed harshly. "Then don't look, sonny, 'cause we're sure as hell goin' to stretch this bastard's neck."

"I tell you I didn't do it!" the prisoner repeated, desperation making his voice quiver. "I just come up here to look for some strays." He looked imploringly at Travers again. "Please help me, mister. I was just doin' what Mr. Pritchard told me to do."

Travers stiffened in the saddle. Buckston turned slightly and barked. "Quit your whinin', Hewett. Galen Pritchard may be a thief and a damn fool, but he ain't stupid. His spread is clear on t'other side of La Junta. Ain't none of his beeves strayed up here on my land, and he knows it."

So the prisoner rode for Milburn Pritchard's son. Travers didn't like the sound of this. He said, "Could be the man's telling the truth, Mr. Buckston. Did you see him changing brands or driving off any of your stock?"

Buckston frowned. One of his riders said suddenly, "Are we goin' to keep listenin' to this feller, Mr. Buckston, or are we goin' to get on with what we was doin'?"

The rancher turned an angry glare toward him. "Whatever we do, Dawson, it'll be because I decide we'll do it. You understand that?"

The cowboy muttered an apology and backed his horse up a step. Buckston turned back to Travers and went on, "I've already wasted enough of my time, Travers. I don't owe you no answers."

"You don't have any proof, do you?" Travers said quickly. "You just saw this man riding on your range and decided he had to be a rustler because he works for this Pritchard."

"That's the way it looks to me," Buckston replied, his voice indignant.

Travers shook his head. "Then this isn't justice, Mr. Buckston. It's murder, pure and simple."

And he was being a fool, Travers thought. There were a dozen cowhands turning angry looks toward him, ready to string him up, too, if their boss gave them the word. There had been a point when he might have been able to turn and ride away from this without any trouble, but he had pushed things beyond that point.

"Listen, son," Buckston said, obviously trying to be reasonable. "You've admitted this ain't any of your business. Just ride on out while you still can. I won't let my boys bother you. But if you keep pushin' in where you ain't wanted, I can't be responsible."

"I can't let you hang this man," Travers replied quietly.

He saw the movement out of the corner of his eye, heard one of Buckston's punchers curse as he yanked his gun from its holster. Travers twisted in the saddle, and suddenly his own Colt was in his hand, roaring just as the other man cleared leather.

The bullet passed close by the cowboy's head, close enough for him to feel the wind of it on his face. He stopped his own draw in midmotion as he found himself staring down the barrel of Travers's gun.

"Drop the gun," Travers told him.

"Hold it!" Buckston roared as more of his men reached for their weapons. Several of the horses, spooked by the shot, took nervous steps.

Travers knew they could cut him to ribbons if they wanted. There was no way he could down more than a couple of them before he was blasted out of the saddle. But for some reason, the prospect didn't seem to worry him too much. Whatever happened would happen. That was simple enough.

Buckston said, "The man told you to drop your gun, Chaney. Reckon you'd better do it."

The cowboy who had started to draw took a deep breath. His fingers uncurled from the butt of his pistol, and it dropped to the dirt with a thump. The glare he directed at Travers was a mixture of hate and fear.

"I don't want a bunch of shootin'," Buckston said wearily. "You willin' to die for a man you never saw before, Travers?"

Slowly, Travers nodded. He couldn't explain it, but he said, "Reckon I am."

"Then you're pure-dee crazy, and I ain't messin' with no crazy man." The rancher turned to look at one of his men and ordered, "Cut Hewett down."

"But, boss—" the puncher started to protest.

"I said cut him down!"

Sweat bathed Hewett's face and he took several deep gulps of relief when the noose around his neck was removed and his hands were cut loose. His body seemed to go limp as the tension of terror left it. He caught himself on the pommel of his saddle as he started to fall.

Buckston yanked his horse around and rode over beside Hewett. "You get off my range," Buckston said in a low, deadly voice. "Happen I should find you on my land again, I won't try to hang you. I'll just shoot you right where you stand. You hear me, boy?"

Hewett nodded jerkily.

Buckston looked back at Travers. "You could've killed Chaney there when he drew on you, couldn't you?"

Travers nodded. "I suppose I could have. And the rest of you would've killed me and then gone on with your hanging. It's better all around this way. Nobody dies."

"We'll see," Buckston grated. Abruptly, he put the spurs to his horse and galloped away. His men fell in behind him, all of them casting hate-filled glances at Travers as they rode off.

Travers holstered his gun and took a deep breath. Looking up at the top of the hill, he saw the wagon come into view. Pritchard had had the sense to wait until Buckston and his men had ridden away before putting in an appearance, and Travers was grateful for that.

He rode over next to Hewett. The man was still leaning on his saddle and breathing heavily. He glanced up at Travers and tried to smile weakly.

"I . . . I can't tell you how obliged I am to you, mister," Hewett said.

Travers looked intently at him. "Were you really rustling Buckston's cattle, Hewett?"

Hewett shook his head vehemently. "I was tellin' the truth. I never stole no cows in my life."

Travers doubted that. It was a rare cowhand who didn't steal a few head from time to time. He said, "You work for Galen Pritchard, do you?"

"Yes, sir. You know Mr. Pritchard?"

"Never had the pleasure." Travers nodded toward the wagon coming down the hill. "But the folks I've been riding with are headed for his ranch. Reckon you can show us the way?"

Hewett stared in surprise at the medicine wagon as it approached. He squinted and moved his lips as he tried to read the writing on its sides. "Doctor . . . Milburn . . . Pritchard," he said. His eyes widened. "Hell, is that feller related to the boss?"

Travers nodded. "His pa."

Hewett stared in appreciation at Leanne Covington. "Don't recollect Mr. Pritchard ever sayin' anything about havin' a sister."

Travers ignored the comment. Leanne was going to create quite a stir when they reached Galen Pritchard's ranch. From the looks of things, these parts were in enough of an uproar already. It appeared that Galen and Buckston were at each other's throats. Travers had heard plenty of stories about range wars and the bloody violence they could create.

And it looked like he had just ridden smack-dab into the middle of one.

Pritchard hauled the wagon to a stop and hopped down from the seat. He hurried over to Travers and Hewett. "Are you all right, my good man?" he anxiously asked the puncher.

Hewett nodded. "Reckon so, thanks to your friend here."

"What the devil was that all about?"

Hewett glanced at Travers, who said, "We're on the range of a man named Buckston, Doc. He seems to be having some kind of feud with the man Hewett here rides for." Travers hesitated. "Hewett works for your son, Galen."

Pritchard shot a startled glance at the still-sweating cowboy. "Is that so? Well, quite a stroke of luck all around, what? You save Mr., ah, Hewett's life, and he can take us to Galen's ranch."

"I'd surely be glad to do that, mister," Hewett said. He swung down from his saddle and bent to pick up a battered hat from the ground. Instead of putting it on, he held it in his hands and nodded to Leanne.

Travers performed the introduction that the puncher was obviously hoping for. "This is Miss Leanne Covington, Hewett." He didn't try to explain what the girl was doing here, since he wasn't completely clear on that himself.

Hewett nodded again. "I'm right pleased to meet you, ma'am," he said.

"Mr. Hewett," Leanne replied coolly, no expression on her face. To look at her, you would never know what a state she had been in when she first saw the near-hanging.

Travers said, "You feel up to riding now, Hewett? I figure we've still got a ways to go."

Hewett wiped the back of his hand across his mouth. "I reckon I'm ready. My nerves are still pretty well shot, but I can ride."

Pritchard smiled and took a bottle of elixir from his coat pocket. "I have just the thing to put you right, my friend. This tonic will soothe your nerves and put new energy in your step."

Hewett looked dubiously at the Englishman. "No hard feelin's, Doc, but I've seen some fellers get messed up something fierce by that snake oil."

"This is not snake oil, dear boy," Pritchard replied easily. "It is instead a genuine medical concoction consisting of only the purest, most healthful ingredients. Why, I prescribe it for myself on a regular basis, as Mr. Travers here can attest." Pritchard held up a finger. "And I'm not trying to sell it to you. I offer it as a gift to one of my son's loyal employees."

"Well, in that case . . ." Hewett licked his lips and reached out from the bottle. "Wouldn't want to hurt nobody's feelin's." He took a long pull, shuddered, and grinned for the first time since Travers had interrupted the hanging. "Hey, that ain't bad!"

"Indeed not." Pritchard climbed back onto the wagon seat and took up the reins. He looked over at Travers. "Shall we proceed?"

"Yep," Travers replied. "Come on, Hewett."

Travers kept his eyes open as the small procession headed southward. For all of his arrogance and abrasiveness, Buckston had not struck him as the kind of man who would wait in ambush for an enemy, but Travers wasn't going to take a chance on riding blind into a trap. Considering the slim possibility that Dale Sorenson was still behind them somewhere, Travers was starting to feel a little penned in. It wasn't a pleasant feeling.

The sun was nearly down when they entered a little valley. The last of the red rays sparkled on a small stream bordered with cottonwoods. The creek ran through the center of the valley, and on its banks a couple of miles ahead, the settlement of La Junta sat, looking peaceful.

Hewett reined in his horse. "We'd best go around town," he said. "Buckston's liable to be there, him and his men. There could be trouble."

Travers nodded. "Sounds like a good idea. You can find your spread all right in the dark?"

"Sure," Hewett snorted. "I know all the trails round here, day or night. It won't be no trouble to get you there."

Travers had intended to make camp tonight and push on to Galen Pritchard's spread the next day, but if Hewett could guide them there was no point in waiting. And the sooner they reached the ranch, the sooner he could push on to other places. The doctor and Leanne would be all right.

"Let's keep rolling, then," Travers said.

They skirted La Junta to the east; Hewett said the trail was easier that way. To the west of town the hills were more rugged, lifting into a small range of mountains. It was pretty good country, Travers thought as dusk closed in. There was enough grass to raise stock. He had been able to tell from the dust and the sparse vegetation in places, though, that there was a delicate balance at work here. A drought, or anything else that would affect that creek, could cause a lot of trouble in this country.

The lights of the town fell behind them. Hewett proved to be right about the trail. It was easy to follow, even by moonlight. The miles rolled on, and Travers's stomach told him that they had skipped supper. He didn't want to stop when they were this close to the ranch. When asked, Hewett said that Galen Pritchard's headquarters was only a couple of miles farther on.

That couple of miles seemed to take a long time to cover, but finally another light came into view. As the wagon and the riders approached, Travers saw that the glow came from one of the windows of a long, low structure with several trees around it. The look of it was Spanish, he noted, with a tile roof over adobe walls. Off to one side was another building, this one made of rough planks, which was undoubtedly the bunkhouse. He saw a small cookshack out back of the main house. There was a well next to the cookshack.

All in all, Galen Pritchard's ranch looked like a mighty nice spread to Travers. He had never felt the desire to settle down and become a stockman, but if he had, he could have done a lot worse than a place like this.

Riding next to the wagon, he said to Pritchard, "Looks like your son has done all right for himself."

The Englishman nodded. "Galen's letters have always been optimistic. I see now he had good cause to feel so."

Hewett said proudly, "The UJ is the best spread in the territory, Doc."

"UJ? I'm afraid I don't understand.

Travers explained. "I reckon that's your son's brand. That'd be the name the ranch is known by."

"That's right," Hewett confirmed. "Named it after the Union Jack, he did. Reckon the boy's've got it hauled in now since it's night, but during the day the boss flies that Britisher flag over the house. That and Old Glory."

Flying the American flag was probably Pritchard's concession to his neighbors, Travers thought. He didn't know what had caused the trouble between Pritchard and Buckston, but a strong display of English pride might have been part of it. Folks in these parts tended not to like outsiders sometimes, which had never made a whole hell of a lot of sense to Travers. Forty or fifty years earlier, *any* white man in this territory would have been an outsider.

As the group passed a small stand of trees a couple of hundred yards away from the house, a voice called out, "Hold on there! Rein in that wagon!"

Pritchard hauled back on the lines as Travers and Hewett brought their mounts to a stop. Travers's first instinct was to reach for his gun, but he had recognized the dangerous tone in those orders, the tone that said they were backed up by a well-aimed Winchester, more than likely.

"It's all right, Ferdy," Hewett called out. "It's me, Hewett. These folks are lookin' for the boss."

The unseen guard replied, "You sure of 'em, Hewett?"

The cowboy laughed harshly. "Hell, I ought to be. One of 'em stopped Buckston from stretchin' my neck, and this feller on the wagon's the boss's pa."

A dark shape emerged from under the trees. The man carried a rifle, just as Travers had guessed. "What'd you say about Buckston?"

Hewett waved off the question. "Never mind. I'll tell you about it later. Is the boss in the house?"

"Yeah. Leastways I think so."

Hewett nodded. He turned to Travers and said, "We'll ride on in. The boys know nobody'd get past Ferdy here without an uproar unless they were friends."

Travers motioned for Pritchard to start the team moving again. It was hard to tell in the moonlight, but he thought he could see the weariness on Leanne's face. It had been a long day.

As they approached the ranch house, Travers thought about what he had seen and heard. The place might look peaceful enough on the surface, just like La Junta did, but it had the same atmosphere of lurking trouble, as if violence could break out at any second. It was a little like riding into an armed camp.

The wagon pulled up in front of the doorway of the house. There was an iron gate across the arched entrance, and inside would be a small patio with the rest of the house built around it.

Travers saw movement in the shadows on the other side of the gate. Suddenly the barrel of a Winchester was thrust through the wrought-iron bars, and it was pointed right at Travers.

"Don't move or I'll blow you out of the saddle," said a voice that retained traces of an English accent.

"Galen!" Pritchard exclaimed. He dropped the reins and stood up on the wagon. His voice shook slightly with emotion. "Galen, it's me."

"Father?" The stunned whisper came from the man holding the rifle. The barrel was pulled back, and its owner suddenly thrust open the gate and all but ran out. "Father, is it really you?"

Pritchard leaped down from the wagon and opened his arms.

The other man hesitated for an instant, then handed the rifle to another shadowy figure who had appeared behind him from the patio. Galen Pritchard rushed forward into his father's arms, both men laughing and slapping each other on the back in what struck Travers as a surprisingly open display of affection.

Travers glanced at the man who had followed Galen out of the courtyard and taken the rifle from him. Abruptly, he frowned. Although the man was still in shadows, there was something familiar about his burly shape.

The man took a step forward, bringing his face into the moonlight. The silvery illumination reflected from the thick, rimless spectacles he wore. Travers suddenly felt cold all over.

"Travers?" Emory Moore said, sounding just as shocked as the man on horseback felt.

Chapter Nine

Travers stared down at the big man for a long moment without speaking. Finally he said in a voice that sounded strange to him, "Howdy, Emory. Didn't expect to see you here."

Emory nodded. "I'm ridin' for Mr. Pritchard now. What brings you here?"

"I ran into the doc there back up the trail and just sort of rode along with him." Travers didn't say anything else. He could see the puzzled look on Emory's face and knew that he was wondering what had happened after the botched-up robbery in Grady. Travers had a feeling Emory hadn't told Galen Pritchard about *that* when he signed on.

The family reunion was still going on beside the wagon. With his hands on his father's shoulders, Galen said, "Emory, bring a lantern. You and Hewett can unload the wagon and bring my father's things inside."

"Yes, sir," Emory replied. With another glance up at Travers, he turned away and went back into the house to fetch the lantern.

"And who is this?" Galen asked as he reached up to help

Leanne down from the seat. "Surely not the little serving girl you mentioned in your letters from London, Father!"

"Leanne is my assistant now," Pritchard told him. "Miss Leanne Covington, this is my son, Galen Pritchard."

"I'm pleased to meet you, Mr. Pritchard," Leanne murmured. "The doctor has spoken of you a great deal."

Galen laughed as he shook Leanne's hand. "No doubt telling you what a scoundrel I was as a boy! Welcome to the UJ Ranch, Miss Covington." He turned back to Pritchard and slapped his father on the back. "What say we all go inside and have some tea?"

"That sounds like an excellent idea, Galen, but there's someone else I want you to meet first." Pritchard led his son over to Travers, who was dismounting from his horse. "This is Mr. Jacob Travers, who was kind enough to rescue us from a spot of difficulty and then accompany us on the rest of our journey."

Emory Moore reappeared from the house, carrying a lantern in his hand. The yellow glow from it washed over Galen Pritchard as he extended his hand to Travers. "So glad to meet you, Mr. Travers," Galen said heartily. "I appreciate you helping my father and Miss Covington."

"My pleasure," Travers grunted as he returned the rancher's hard grip.

The light from the lantern gave Travers his first good look at Galen. He was young, thirty perhaps, and had striking good looks. His crisp blond hair and ready smile probably had all the ladies in La Junta charmed.

Galen wore a brown shirt and tan pants tucked into high black boots. There was no gun belt around his waist, but he had handled the Winchester with practiced ease. Travers had a feeling he was tougher than he looked.

Emory didn't look at Travers as he and Hewett began taking bags from the wagon. Milburn Pritchard pointed out which valises he and Leanne would want unloaded, and Galen took the lantern while the two men carried the bags through the gate. "Put my father's things in the room next to mine," Galen called after them. "Miss Covington will have the east bedroom. When you're finished, put the wagon in the stable and tend to the horses, will you?"

"Sure thing, Mr. Pritchard," Emory replied over his shoulder.

Travers noticed that Hewett hadn't said anything to Galen about the trouble with Buckston and his men. Probably didn't want to upset the guests, he decided. Despite the fact that they had been in this country for a couple of years, Pritchard and Leanne seemed a little naive.

"Well, come along, come along," Galen said. "You, too, Mr. Travers. Or would you prefer to see to your own horse and gear?"

"I'll be along," Travers said. He didn't want Emory Moore handling his horse. He wasn't sure just yet how he felt about Emory, but the image of the big man riding hell-for-leather out of Grady and leaving him behind was still strong in Travers's mind.

Emory had also been his friend. Travers told himself not to judge anybody too harshly. Jumping to conclusions was part of what had started him on the outlaw trail.

He seemed to have left that trail now, he thought as he led his horse toward the stable near the bunkhouse. Galen called after him, "Come along inside when you're settled in, Mr. Travers." Travers made no reply except a wave.

Galen hadn't offered him a room in the main house, and that was all right with Travers. He could bunk with the hands for the one night he was planning to be here. Hell, he could sleep in the barn with his horse if it came to that. Wouldn't be the first night he'd spent in such surroundings—or a lot worse.

A middle-aged, stove-up wrangler was sleeping in a chair leaning against the wall just inside the stable. The man snored and snorted and let the chair come down with a thump as Travers led his horse inside. He stood up wearily, blinking his eyes in the feeble light of a lantern that was about to run out of kerosene.

"Who the hell're you?" he demanded.

"Name's Travers. Your boss told me I could put my horse up."

The wrangler waved a hand. "Find you a empty stall. There're a few. Grain in the bin there, water in the bucket. Less'n you'd rather me do it."

"No, old-timer, I can handle it," Travers grinned. The wrangler was clean-shaven, but with his leathery face and gnarled figure, he reminded Travers somewhat of old George back at Ghost River.

He unsaddled the horse, rubbed him down, let him drink a little, and gave him some feed. It was a familiar ritual, and Travers could do it without thinking. He was pondering what he should do about Emory Moore when a footstep sounded behind him on the hard-packed dirt floor.

"Sure as hell didn't expect to run into you again this soon," Emory said.

Travers turned slowly, not sure whether to be angry. He said, "I didn't expect to find you working as a ranch hand, either, Emory."

The big man leaned against the side of the stall in the deceptive slouch that Travers remembered. Emory looked lazy and sleepy and maybe a little dumb, and he was none of those things. Travers had seen him explode into violence from that position on more than one occasion.

Emory glanced at the front of the barn, where the wrangler had settled down in his chair and started snoring again. "Reckon I ought to say thanks." His voice was quiet, low-pitched. "You sure saved my bacon back there in Grady."

"Forget it," Travers said harshly. He bent and picked up his saddle, looking for a sawhorse.

Emory reached out and put a big hand on Travers's arm. "I thought you were a goner, Jacob," he said earnestly. "I saw you go down, and I figured there was no way you were getting up again. Didn't see any reason for both of us to die there just because Lobo lied to us about where he'd been."

"You ran out on me."

"I thought you were going to *die*."

Travers studied his former partner's face in the lanternlight. "Would you have come back if you'd known I was going to make it?"

"Hell, yes, I would have! A man don't run out on a pard. You know that."

Travers knew it, all right. And he heard nothing but sincerity in Emory's voice. But somehow he wasn't sure if he believed what the big man was telling him.

Still, it was all over now. They were both alive, and from the looks of things, they had both made fresh starts. Travers had already exposed his own past to Pritchard and Leanne, but he doubted Emory had done likewise with Galen. It would serve no real purpose for him to go around pointing fingers, Travers decided.

"It's over and done with," he grunted. "Let's leave it that way."

Emory looked relieved. "Sure, Travers. And thanks. Mr. Pritchard's been good to me so far. I'd hate for him to know I used to be an owlhoot."

"He won't hear it from me." Travers dropped his saddle on a sawhorse in the corner of the stable and started toward the entrance. Emory fell in beside him. As they emerged into the cool night air, Travers went on, "I didn't know you were ever a cowhand."

Emory grinned. "I've done most everything in my time, boy. A man gets along better if he can turn his hand to different things. Don't reckon Pritchard hired me just to punch cattle, though." He chuckled. "Come on. I'll walk with you up to the house."

One of those uneasy feelings passed through Travers again. "What's your job, then?" he asked.

Emory seemed to ignore the question for the moment. "Hewett was telling me while we carried in the bags that you saved him from one of Buckston's necktie parties."

Travers nodded. "Buckston claimed he was rustling."

"Buckston'd say anything to justify stringing up a UJ rider. He and Pritchard don't get along no how, no way."

"Has it come down to shooting yet?"

Emory shook his head. "Not yet. But it's going to. And when it does, I'll really start earning my money from Pritchard."

"You've hired out your gun, you mean."

"Nothing wrong with that. Men do it all the time."

Travers nodded. It made sense now. Emory was fast enough to hold his own with most men, and he'd be a good one to have on your side in a range war.

"You ever give any thought to going into that line of work yourself?" Emory asked now. "I reckon I could use another good man to side me in this fight."

I'll just bet you could, Travers thought. *Somebody to save your hide and get gunned down in your place. . . .*

"I'm not a gunfighter," he said flatly. "And I want no part of any trouble between Pritchard and Buckston. I already mixed in more than I should have. I'm riding on south in the morning."

Emory shrugged his wide shoulders. "The offer's open if you're interested." He chuckled. "Say, you remember that time I told Sam I had a gal for him in that line shack up Wyoming way? And instead it was a big silvertip grizzly waitin' in there for him?"

Travers had to smile a little at the memory. "I remember," he said. "Sam came out of there in one hell of a hurry."

Emory's laughter boomed. "He sure did."

Sam had been sporting a pretty funny expression at the time, Travers thought. That was just like Emory. You never knew what you were letting yourself in for when you listened to him.

Emory swung open the iron gate at the house and stepped back to let Travers enter first. Travers heard the sound of laughter from the other side of the patio. Through an open door in one of the thick adobe walls, he could see Pritchard and Galen and Leanne standing and drinking something from cups.

"I'll be headin' on back to the bunkhouse," Emory said. "Reckon you'll be in good hands." He waved and strolled off into the darkness.

Travers watched him go, then shook his head. Emory Moore was a hard man to figure.

As Travers entered the room, Galen spotted him and said, "Ah, there you are, Mr. Travers. Would you care for a spot of tea?"

Travers shook his head. "No, thanks."

"You see, Galen, I told you he wasn't the type of man who drinks tea," Pritchard said.

"Whiskey, then?" Galen suggested.

Travers let himself smile slightly. "How about a beer?"

"That we can do." Galen reached over and tugged on a bell pull that was hanging on one wall. "Rosita!" he called.

A moment later an elderly Mexican woman appeared in one of the arched doorways that led out of the room. She said, "Yes, Señor Galen?"

"Bring Mr. Travers here a beer," Galen told her. She nodded and shuffled away, returning a moment later with a tall, dark brown bottle.

Travers accepted it with a smile of thanks, then took a pull at the cool liquid inside. Homemade brew, he decided, and quite good. It felt nice going down his throat, cutting the dust of the day's long ride.

He lowered the bottle and took a look around the room. It was big, low-ceilinged, shadowy in the corners. There was an Indian rug on the hardwood floor, and several heavy chairs were scattered around. A massive rolltop desk took up one whole corner. There were papers out on the desktop, an open ledger resting on top of them.

A round chandelier hung from the ceiling and held at least a score of candles, which provided the room's soft light. Three paintings were hung on one wall, countryside scenes that didn't look anything like the terrain in these parts. Travers wondered if they represented places in England. On the opposite wall was another Indian rug, this one like a tapestry.

The remaining wall decorations were more functional—gun racks holding a variety of rifles and shotguns. A tall wooden case with a glass front contained an assortment of handguns. Galen Pritchard had plenty of hardware on hand.

Considering his problems with Buckston, he might need it.

"What do you think of my little hacienda, Mr. Travers?"

Travers looked at Galen Pritchard. "Appears to be a right nice place. In fact, from what I could tell in the dark, it looks like you've got quite a spread."

"Yes, indeed," Galen replied with a smile. "And I've worked hard for it, too, I don't mind saying. This was wild country when I came here ten years ago."

"You must've been pretty young."

"A mere lad he was," Milburn Pritchard put in. "I never wanted him to leave England, but he had his heart set on it. Wanted to see the great new land America, he did."

Galen added, "And from what I saw, there's no better place to settle in the whole country than right here."

Travers drank some more of the good beer. "Place could use a little more water," he observed as he lowered the bottle.

"We have all we need," Galen said. "La Junta Creek has never run dry in the ten years I've been here. It runs along the eastern border of my range and gives us plenty of good grazing land. Of course, my holdings toward the west are rather dry most of the time. It would be better if the creek followed a more central course through the ranch, but one cannot have everything, can one?"

"Never knew anybody who did," Travers answered. He was wondering where Galen had gotten the money to buy a spread like this when he had come into the country as little more than a boy, but it was none of his business. Curiosity was all right; indulging it wasn't.

He looked over at Leanne, who was her usual quiet self. One of these days the girl was going to string more than a couple of sentences together, and he'd fall over from the surprise.

Abruptly, Travers gave a little shake of his head at the thought. He would be long gone by the time *that* happened.

Pritchard moved over beside his son and put his hand on Galen's shoulder again. The pride on his face was obvious. Seeing it, Travers felt a strange pang inside him. He hadn't felt anything quite like it for a long time . . . ever since he had ridden away from his own father.

Away from the old man's preaching and moralizing and judging and betraying—

Travers caught himself and lifted the beer, finishing it off in a couple of deep swallows.

"Shall I have Rosita fetch you another, Mr. Travers?" Galen asked.

Travers shook his head. "Thanks anyway. I think if it's all right with you folks, I'll head out to the bunkhouse and get some sleep." He put the empty bottle on a table and started to turn away.

Galen's hand on his arm stopped him. When Travers glanced back, there was a solemn expression on the rancher's smooth face. "My father told me what happened with Hewett," Galen said. "Facing down Buckston and his hired guns was a brave thing to do."

"Or a stupid one," Travers told him bluntly. He hadn't planned to bring up the subject, but he supposed that deep down he had known they would have to talk about it. "But it seemed like the thing to do at the time. I didn't want to see an innocent man dancing on air. Goes against the grain."

"Indeed. I want to thank you for coming to Hewett's assistance. I daresay you saved his life." Angry lights glittered in Galen's blue eyes. "Buckston and his rascals would have enjoyed watching him hang, I believe."

"They claimed he was rustling."

Galen shook his head. "Nothing of the sort. Some of my cattle strayed, and I sent Hewett up there to see if they might have wandered onto Buckston's range."

Travers remembered Buckston saying that Galen Pritchard was

no fool, but now the man was starting to sound a little like one. "That's a long way for cows to stray," Travers said. "Clear on the other side of La Junta, in fact."

"Yes, but what Buckston may perhaps be unaware of is that my range now extends into that part of the county. Until recently my northern boundaries were roughly the same latitude as the town, although west of there, of course. But since I've purchased a smaller ranch from a man named Demeter, my holdings are now adjacent to Buckston's. I've been moving cattle onto that range for over a week."

Travers frowned. "And you didn't tell Buckston about it?"

"I saw no need to. It was, after all, a transaction between Arthur Demeter and myself. Mr. Buckston had no part in it."

"He may see it different. From the way he sounded, I don't think he wants you as a neighbor, Mr. Pritchard." Travers didn't want to be rude to his host, but obviously somebody needed to set Galen straight about a few things.

"That's as may be, but the deal is closed. That's my range now, and I intend to use it." There was an undertone of steel in Galen's voice. He could be a stubborn man when he wanted to, Travers realized.

"Here now, we simply cannot discuss cattle all night," Pritchard put in. "We have a great deal of catching up to do, Galen."

"Yes, of course." The pleasant expression was back on Galen's face. "But we don't want to bore Miss Covington or Mr. Travers with our reminiscences, Father."

"Don't worry about me," Leanne said. "If someone will show me to my room, I think I'd like to retire."

"Certainly. Rosita!"

When the wizened little servant had led Leanne away through one of the doors, Travers said, "I was on my way out, too. You folks enjoy your talk."

"Good night, Mr. Travers," Galen said. "I hope you sleep well, and remember, my home is your home."

"Thank you," Travers nodded. He started for the door again.

This time it was Milburn Pritchard who stopped him by stepping quickly after him. He seized Travers's hand and looked intently at him. "I do want to thank you, Mr. Travers. I don't think we would have made it here if it had not been for you."

Remembering the Sorenson brothers, Travers had a feeling Pritchard was correct. But right now, all he wanted was some sleep. After that some breakfast and an open trail in front of him. . . .

He made it out the door before either of them could stop him again.

Weariness had a tight hold on him as he crossed the patio and then walked over to the bunkhouse. A lantern was still lit there, and as he neared the open door, he could hear the soft murmur of men's voices. He paused in the doorway.

He'd never worked as a cowhand, so he couldn't say if this was a typical bunkhouse or not. It was long and narrow, with a double row of bunks separated by an aisle where several men stood lounging and smoking. At the far end of the room, in an open area, were a couple of rough tables. Both of them were in use at the moment. A pair of card games were in progress. The chairs around the tables were all full, and several more punchers watched from the sides, probably waiting for a spot to open up. Most of the men who weren't either playing cards or observing the games were sitting on their bunks and repairing boots or holsters. There was a feeling of friendship in the air along with the blue haze of smoke from a dozen quirlies.

Friendship or not, Travers suddenly realized, he would go crazy if he had to come back to the same place every night for weeks and months on end. He supposed he had always been a fiddlefoot; the last two years had just made him more set in his ways.

Emory Moore was one of the men playing cards. He looked up, spotted Travers in the doorway, and threw in his hand after glancing at the pasteboards one more time. "Ain't worth it," he declared. He got to his feet and started toward Travers. Another man slipped into his place.

"Reckon a man could find a place to sleep around here?" Travers asked. Emory pointed out a vacant bunk.

"How long you been here, Emory? A week?" Travers had lost track of time to a certain extent. His memory seemed to be playing tricks on him. He couldn't recollect exactly how long he had been at Ghost River with George.

"Hell, nigh onto a month, I'd say. But however long it's been, I know this is a good place, Travers. The pay's just fine, and Pritchard's trying to really make something out of this ranch."

"I'd say he already has."

"It's big, all right. But it's going to get bigger."

Travers tossed his hat onto the rough bed to let any other homeless strays who might wander in know that it was taken. He went back out to the stable long enough to fetch his warbag off his saddle. By the time he returned to the bunkhouse, the card games were breaking up and the punchers were turning toward their beds.

Emory came over and said good night. Travers grunted, pulled off his boots and shirt and pants, and settled down on the bunk as one of the punchers blew out the lantern. Morning always came early on a ranch, and within moments the sounds of snoring and deep, regular breathing filled the long room.

Travers couldn't fall asleep right away, despite the fatigue that gripped him. He kept seeing in his mind's eye that scene in the clearing when the man called Hewett had come mighty damn close to dying.

And now that he knew what had been behind this incident, he didn't feel any easier in his mind. There had probably been friction between Galen and Buckston for years, and now the young Englishman was going to aggravate it by buying a spread next to Buckston and moving his cattle onto it.

It didn't make any sense. From what Travers had seen of that country in the distance, the Demeter place didn't look anywhere near as good as the range that Galen already had. It was brown and gray to the eye instead of green, which meant that it was dry and rocky. There was probably enough graze there to run a few head of stock, but why bother? Galen already had plenty of range that was watered by La Junta Creek.

Travers rolled onto his side and forced himself to close his eyes. There was no figuring some people. Galen had to have some reason for doing what he was doing. Whatever the reason, he and Buckston would just have to work out their problems by themselves.

Because, come tomorrow night, Jacob Travers was going to be a long way on down the trail.

Chapter Ten

Once he finally dozed off, Travers slept better than he had expected to. He had no dreams, at least none that he remembered, and when he awoke in the morning, he felt rested and ready to go.

The hands were already up and gone, and bright sunlight slanted in through the bunkhouse windows. Evidently he had been so tired that he had slept right through the inevitable commotion as the other men got up and went about their business.

After he had dressed, Travers found a pump by the well and doused his head, shaking the cold droplets out of his long hair and then putting on his hat. There was smoke coming from the chimney of the little cookshack. The cook was probably already preparing the noon meal, but with any luck Travers knew he could still scrounge some breakfast. He headed in that direction.

Before he reached the cookshack, Galen Pritchard emerged from the house and spotted him. "Ah, good morning!" the Englishman said exuberantly. "I trust you slept well, Mr. Travers?"

"Just fine," Travers nodded.

"I realized after you had retired last night that I should have offered you the hospitality of the house. Anyone who was as helpful to my father as you've been shouldn't have had to sleep in a bunkhouse."

Travers shook his head. "Don't worry about that. That bunkhouse was downright swell to somebody who's slept on as much hard ground as I have."

"Well, I'm glad you were able to get some rest. Now, come on into the house. I instructed Rosita to save some breakfast for you and keep it warm."

"Mighty nice of you." Travers let Galen lead him into the rambling adobe house. He hadn't seen the dining room the night before, but in the morning light that came through its big windows, it was as impressive as the rest of the place, with a long table of polished mahogany and heavy chairs. Galen had to be doing pretty well financially with the ranch to be able to afford all this finery.

Travers put away a steak, a pile of hotcakes, and several biscuits dripping with butter. The coffee was strong and black, the way he liked it. Galen Pritchard knew how to make a man feel at home.

Actually, Travers mused, this was a hell of a lot nicer than anything he'd ever gotten in his own home.

Galen sat down across the table from him and sipped on a cup of coffee. After a few moments, he said, "Excellent fare, isn't it?"

"Mighty good," Travers allowed.

"Rosita and her daughter Felicia are very good cooks. Their meals are only one of the advantages to working here, Mr. Travers."

Travers glanced up at him, eyes narrowing. "Sounds like Emory Moore has been talking to you."

Galen nodded. "He did recommend that I speak to you about possible employment. He said you were a good man."

Travers glanced around the room. He and Galen were the only ones here, Rosita having left the room after serving the food. "Where's your pa this morning?"

"One of the hands is showing him the remuda. Father certainly appreciates good horses, and we have some of the best animals in the territory here on the UJ."

"And Miss Covington?"

Galen shook his head. "I'm not sure. Perhaps she's with Rosita and Felicia. You haven't responded to the suggestion that you go to work for me, Mr. Travers."

"I wanted to be able to talk plain, Mr. Pritchard, and I'm not sure your pa and Miss Covington really understand the West yet."

Galen waved a hand. "By all means, sir, speak your mind."

"This trouble you've been having with Buckston is going to get worse. You know it, and your men know it."

"If Mr. Buckston will only be reasonable—"

"He's not going to," Travers cut in. "Not as long as he thinks you're trying to move onto his range. And buying that Demeter place and moving stock onto it is surely going to look like a push to Buckston."

Galen said, "There's nothing wrong with wanting to expand my holdings."

Travers grinned. "Reckon there isn't. No matter how much folks have, it's usually not enough. All I'm saying is that if you push Buckston, he's going to push back. And then you'll have a shooting war on your hands, sure as hell."

Frowning across the table, Galen Pritchard said, "Suppose I concede your point, Mr. Travers. What does this have to do with my asking you to work for me?"

"I've never punched cattle in my life," Travers said flatly. "That leaves just one reason you'd want to hire me. And my gun's not for sale, either."

"Not even to help protect innocent people?"

"I don't need pay for that. But you don't need me here, either." Travers looked at the empty plate in front of him and sighed. "Mighty good food, all right. But I'll still be pushing on."

"I wish I could convince you otherwise."

Travers shoved his chair back and stood up. "I'm obliged to you for the bunk and the grub, Mr. Pritchard. But I'll be saddling up now."

Galen got to his feet and fell in beside him as Travers left the dining room and crossed the living room to the patio. "If you change your mind," the rancher said, "I'm sure there will always be a place for you here, Mr. Travers. I think my father and Leanne will miss you."

Travers paused at the wrought-iron gate. "They're staying on?"

"Yes, of course. Why shouldn't they?"

"I had the idea they were just here for a visit." Travers shrugged. "That's all. I didn't think your pa was ready to give up selling that elixir."

Galen laughed. "My father is no longer a young man, despite his vigor. It's time he settled down. He's going to get in trouble if he keeps wandering about the frontier like he has the last two years."

Travers glanced at the other man. "He tell you about what was going on when I ran into him and the girl?"

"About those loutish brothers? What was their name, Sorenson? Yes, he did indeed tell me. That's just the sort of thing I'm talking about when I say he would be better off to give up the wandering life."

"The rest of the Sorensons are liable to show up here one of these days."

Galen shook his head. "I'm not worried about that, Mr. Travers. My men and I will set them straight."

Travers saw the rancher's point. Emory wasn't the only gunhand among the crew. Dale Sorenson and his other brothers would be fools to try to start trouble on the UJ Ranch.

"Still, you keep your eyes open for those boys." He started toward the stable to get his horse ready to travel.

"Stop back by the house before you leave," Galen called after him. Travers nodded and waved a hand.

His horse had already been fed and watered this morning,

Travers saw when he checked on the animal. He moved into the stall and stroked the horse's flank, murmuring, "You're enjoying all this rest and good grub, aren't you, old boy? Wish we could stay awhile for your sake, but I reckon we'd best be moving on."

From behind him, Leanne Covington said, "I wish you wouldn't."

Travers spun around, instinct making his hand start toward the gun on his hip. He stopped the draw in midmotion before his fingers grasped the walnut butt of the Colt. Leanne took an involuntary step back when she saw the violence of his reaction and the intensity on his face.

Travers forced himself to relax and shake his head. "I slept too long and ate too good," he muttered. "Must've stopped up my ears. I should have heard you coming, ma'am. Sorry I scared you."

Leanne shook her head. "I'm the one who should apologize. I suppose I'm in the habit of walking softly. But I knew better than to come up behind you like that."

The soft lilt of her slightly accented voice made Travers want to smile. She looked awfully pretty this morning, her dark hair shining, wearing a different dress than any of the ones he had seen before. This one was blue, with tiny white flowers on it and a lace-trimmed neckline that dropped a little lower than he was used to. There was a little white bow in the center of the neckline.

He turned back to the horse, not wanting to look at her anymore and get distracted from what he was doing. "You looking for me?" he asked over his shoulder.

"Yes, I was. Galen Pritchard told me that you're leaving."

"Reckon I am."

"I thought you might stay on for a while here at the ranch."

Travers shook his head. "Don't recollect ever saying I was planning to do that. I appreciated sleeping in a bed for a change last night, but now it's time to ride."

"On down the trail, is that it?"

Travers had to look at her when he heard the touch of bitterness in her voice. "That's right," he said.

"You're what do they call it, faddlefooted?"

"Fiddlefooted," he corrected. "I suppose so."

"Never stay in one place long enough to care about anything, I assume?"

What the hell was going on here? She sounded mad at him about something. What did she care if he rode out? They had been barely polite to each other during the journey down here. He couldn't believe that she was going to miss him when he was gone.

"I don't want to be rude, Miss Covington, but if you've got something to say to me, why don't you just spit it out?"

"Very well." Her chin lifted. "I don't want you to go. And I'm sure that Dr. Pritchard wouldn't, either. Galen told me that he offered you work and you turned him down. Do you mind telling me why? I imagine he pays quite well."

"Reckon he does. Did he tell you what he'd be paying me for?"

Leanne frowned slightly. "Why, to be a cowboy, I suppose."

Travers hesitated, unsure how much to tell her about how he saw the situation around here. He didn't want to scare her by tossing around words like "range war."

"I think there may be some trouble coming," he finally said. "But it's none of my business, and I don't want to get mixed up in it."

"It was none of your business when those men were trying to harm the doctor and me, either, but that didn't stop you from 'getting mixed up in it,' thank God."

"That was different."

"How?"

"It just was," Travers insisted.

"Well, if you're interested, I think there may be some problems here, too." Leanne looked away, wouldn't meet his eyes. "I . . . I have a bad feeling about this place, Mr. Travers. You may think it's foolish to place any stock in such things, but my mum could always tell when things were going to go wrong. She told me not to go to work for Dr. Pritchard—"

She broke off, probably sensing that she had gone too far and said too much. Despite his intention to leave as soon as possible, Travers had to ask, "You don't like him much, do you?"

Leanne took so long to answer that he was beginning to think she was going to ignore the question. Then, finally, she said, "No, I don't like him much."

"Then why do you stay with him? Why'd you come over here with him in the first place?"

She lifted her head, her gaze boring into his eyes and burning with fires he hadn't seen there before. "Do you have any idea what it is like to be poor, Mr. Travers?"

He snorted. "I've never been rich."

"Yes, but have you been *poor*? Have you been poor in a city where thousands and thousands of others are in just as desperate straits as you and your family? Have you lived in a place where there is hardly room to turn around, to even breathe?"

Travers took a deep breath, surprised by the vehemence of her questions. "No," he said, "I don't reckon I have."

"Well, I have. And I assure you, being a servant for a man like Dr. Pritchard is better than slowly dying in filth and poverty. Even when he . . . he . . ."

The words choked off, and Travers remembered all too well what had gone on in the wagon during the journey. "You don't have to explain," he said harshly. "I'm not your pa."

Leanne looked away and shook her head. "No, you're not. It's none of your business. That's your attitude about nearly everything, isn't it?" She laughed shortly. "At any rate, the rest of my history is very simple. Dr. Pritchard wished to come to America, and he offered to bring me with him. I accepted. I'm here of my own free will, Mr. Travers." She moved a step closer to him. "I can leave whenever I want, go where I please."

Travers didn't say anything for a moment. This was the longest conversation he had ever had with Leanne Covington, and it had sure as hell taken some unexpected turns. Unless he was badly mistaken, she was offering to leave the ranch with him. And the way she moved closer to him, the bold look in her dark eyes, all told him that she had in mind the same sort of relationship she had with Pritchard.

She wanted something from him, and she was ready to use everything she had to get it.

Just like Polly Dawes had wanted something from him.

Travers gave an abrupt shake of his head. "I'm used to riding alone," he said harshly.

There was a quick intake of breath from Leanne. "I see . . . and I'm sorry I bothered you, Mr. Travers." She turned sharply. "I won't detain you any longer."

A part of Travers wanted to reach out and stop her as she marched out of the stable, but he stayed where he was, arms at his sides. The best thing was to let her go and then get the hell out of here himself.

He saddled up quickly and led the horse from the stable. Pausing for a second, he looked through the gate into the patio. Galen Pritchard had told him to stop by the house before he left, but Travers didn't want to. Galen would probably just make another pitch for him to stay. Travers suddenly wondered if the rancher had had anything to do with Leanne coming to the stable and asking him not to leave. He decided he was being too suspicious. Leanne didn't strike him as the type to do Galen Pritchard's dirty work, at least not that kind.

Travers got his warbag from the deserted bunkhouse, swung into the saddle, and put the spurs to the horse. He rode away from the ranch house at a good trot, rapidly putting it behind him.

He had gone less than half a mile when he heard the shots.

Travers stopped his horse and turned in the saddle to look behind him. He had come over a slight rise that kept him from seeing the ranch house, but he could tell that the gunfire was coming from that direction.

Grimacing, Travers sat there for a long moment and listened to the crackle of handguns and the sharper crack of rifles. From the sound of it, there was quite a battle going on back there.

Buckston and his men must have come to call. Travers wondered if Buckston had found out about Galen buying the Demeter place.

If that was the case, the war had begun, all right.

"Damn." The curse was low and heartfelt as it was torn from Travers's mouth.

He turned the horse around and galloped back toward the UJ.

Old George would have been proud of him, he thought fleetingly as his mount raced up the rise. He seemed to get caught up in every lost cause he ran across these days. There had been a time when Jacob Travers wouldn't have even considered risking his own neck to help out somebody else.

He topped the hill and slowed down long enough to take in the scene below. Several saddled horses were milling around near the bunkhouse. Men lay or crouched behind every bit of cover they could find, shooting toward the house. A blue pall of powder smoke already hung over the yard. Return fire came sporadically from the ranch house.

Travers spotted Buckston behind a tree. The old rancher was blazing away at the house with a pistol.

There couldn't be very many people inside. Most, if not all, of Galen's hands were out on the range. In fact, Travers hadn't seen any of them around before he left.

It was possible that the only ones resisting the attack were Galen, his father, Leanne Covington, and the two Mexican servants. Buckston had at least six men with him.

Bad odds. Travers would have to do what he could to even them up.

He rode down the hill, drawing his gun and leaning forward over the horse's neck. He held his fire, even after some of Buckston's men noticed and started throwing shots his way.

Travers let out a yell as his horse thundered through the yard. He raced behind most of Buckston's men, and they had to turn away from the house to deal with his threat. Travers triggered a couple of shots, saw one man clutch a shattered shoulder and stagger away, and watched as another dove for cover as his hat spun off crazily.

Some of Buckston's men exposed themselves to the fire from the house as they concentrated on Travers. One of them suddenly jerked erect, a bloody patch appearing on his chest. As he pitched forward on his face, a matching stain showed on the back of his shirt.

The man had been killed from behind, Travers realized.

By now he was past Buckston's men. He veered to the side, holding the Colt behind him and emptying it in hopes of keeping them occupied rather than hitting anything. As the horse made for the house, Travers kicked his feet out of the stirrups.

He angled the horse more until it was running back in the direction from which he had come, only now the wall of the ranch house was only a few feet away on his right. As the gate into the courtyard flashed by, Travers dropped from the saddle, keeping the horse between him and the enemy guns for the split second it took him to slam the gate open with his shoulder. He was lucky it hadn't been locked, he thought as he fell through the gate and landed heavily. A quick roll put him out of the line of fire, safe behind the thick adobe wall that surrounded the patio.

Riding in like this hadn't been as daring a move as it might appear, he knew. About the only thing harder than hitting a man on a running horse was shooting from the back of such an animal. He had heard a couple of slugs whine by a few feet from his head during the wild dash, but that was as close as any of them had come.

"Travers!"

He looked up as someone called his name, and he saw Galen Pritchard kneeling just inside the doorway of the house, a Winchester in his hands. Travers waved to show that he was all right, then dumped the empties in his Colt and jammed fresh cartridges in their place.

More shots were coming from one of the windows of the house, down the wall several feet from the gate. Somebody else besides Galen was mounting a defense. Doc Pritchard maybe, Travers supposed. He didn't know which of the men in the house had shot Buckston's man in the back.

Travers knew at least two of Buckston's men were out of the fight, but that still left the odds against them. On his belly, he edged to the gate and peered around the corner of the wall long enough to snap another shot at one of the concealed gunmen.

They might not have to hold off Buckston for long. Surely the rest of the hands would hear the gunfire and come running. That would be enough to turn the tide.

And that was exactly what happened a few minutes later. Between blasts, Travers suddenly heard hoofbeats, and within moments Buckston yelled, "Hold your fire! Come on, men!"

Anger gripped Travers. Buckston had been quick to attack a lightly defended house, but now he was going to cut and run as soon as the odds evened up. Travers surged to his feet and ducked through the gate in time to see Buckston and his men hauling themselves into the saddles of their nervous horses.

"Buckston!"

Travers's cry made the burly rancher jerk around in his saddle. Buckston yanked his pistol around, and it belched flame and smoke at the same instant that Travers's gun exploded.

Both men missed. Travers felt the heat of Buckston's slug on his face, and Buckston's horse reared just in time to let Travers's bullet smack past its rider harmlessly. Then Buckston and his men were plunging away at a breakneck gallop, and there was no point in wasting any more lead.

Travers stood with his gun in his hand, gazing after the fleeing men. The group of Galen's cowhands came thundering up to the house, guns out and ready but no longer needed. "What the hell happened?" one of them demanded.

Galen came out of the house, still holding his rifle. Behind him, face drained of color, came Milburn Pritchard. Travers saw that both of them appeared to be unhurt. The third man to come out of the house was a bit of a surprise. Emory Moore held a Winchester, like Galen, and Travers suddenly realized that he must have been the other defender firing from the window down the wall.

Galen answered the cowboy's question. "Buckston and his

men came to pay us a bit of a social call," he said dryly. There was enough of a quiver underneath the words for Travers to hear the anger and fear inside the man.

"He found out you bought that ranch up by his spread, didn't he?" Travers asked.

Galen nodded. "Yes. He had business in La Junta this morning and was told about the sale by the county clerk. He was quite livid about it." The young Englishman put his hand on Travers's shoulder. "It seems you've continued your pattern of assisting the Pritchards in times of dire need, old man. If it hadn't been for you and Emory here, I daresay Buckston would have murdered us all."

Travers holstered his gun. "Is Miss Covington all right?"

Milburn Pritchard spoke up. "Leanne is fine, Mr. Travers. Quite frightened, of course, but unharmed. Rosita is attempting to comfort her at the moment."

Travers glanced at Emory Moore and said, "I didn't know you were anywhere around this morning."

"I rode in just as you were going over that hill," Emory grunted. "I saw you up there and got a mite offended that you'd leave without saying good-bye, pard."

Travers turned his attention back to Galen. He asked, "Did Buckston ride up shooting?"

Galen shook his head. "No, he spent a moment indulging in some of the vilest profanity I've ever heard, along with threats to run me out of the territory and clean back to England." He laughed harshly. "I suppose he'll think twice before trying that again, eh?"

"Who fired the first shot?"

"One of his men, I suppose," Galen shrugged. "I was attempting to reason with the man when the shooting started. One of his hired killers must have gotten impatient. It was all I could do to duck back in the house before I was ventilated, as you westerners say."

Emory was grinning broadly as he looked at Travers. "I knew you'd come back," he said now when Galen paused. "You never could stay out of a good fight, could you, Travers?"

Travers gave a humorless laugh. "It doesn't look like it."

He had solidly aligned himself with Galen Pritchard now. Twice he had opposed Forrest Buckston, and both times he had slung lead at Buckston's men. Buckston wasn't the kind of man to forget that.

"What do you say, Mr. Travers?" Galen went on. "Fate seems to have returned you to us. Will you stay on this time?"

He could still ride out of this part of the country. Buckston had his hands full; he wouldn't spare the time or energy to follow Travers.

But if there was such a thing as fate, then everything sure looked like it intended for him to stay here and take a hand in this fight. Galen, Emory, and Leanne had all asked him to stay. Despite what he had done back in Grady, Emory was a good fighter and the rest of the crew seemed salty enough, but Buckston had them outgunned. And he had an old-timer's stubborn resistance to a newcomer pushing in on his range. To Buckston, Galen would be a newcomer, even though he had been here for ten years.

Buckston was like an old bull who would fight to the death if he was challenged.

All these thoughts raced through Travers's head. Maybe he was making a mistake, he thought as he took a deep breath, but the decision suddenly seemed clear-cut to him.

"I'll play out the hand," he said.

Chapter Eleven

Travers stowed his gear in the bunkhouse again and put his horse back in the stable. Galen had asked him to come into the house when he got settled, so he walked over to the big adobe structure and pushed through the gate. The door into the living room was still open, so he strolled inside, his hat in his hand.

He found Leanne Covington sitting there in one of the heavy armchairs. Her face was pale, and he could tell she was still feeling the effects of the gun battle. He nodded to her and said, "You all right, Miss Covington?"

She looked up at him with slightly glassy eyes, and he suddenly suspected that she had been indulging in some of Pritchard's elixir. "I'm fine," she said, her voice only a little thicker than normal. "Why should I be otherwise?"

"Well, I thought all that shooting might've—"

She cut him off with a sharp wave of her hand. "Shooting? Why, that's something that occurs every day, isn't it, Mr. Travers? Death before noon is quite normal here in the West, is it not?"

"Not always," Travers snapped.

Leanne looked down. "That man was shot in the back," she murmured, more to herself than to him. "Shot down with no mercy."

Seeing that had bothered Travers, too, but he pointed out, "That fella who got killed had been shooting at us just a few seconds before. He wasn't showing a whole hell of a lot of mercy himself."

Leanne didn't respond for a moment. When she finally looked back up at him, she said, "I suppose you're looking for Galen, aren't you?" At Travers's nod, she went on, "He and Dr. Pritchard are in the study. They said for you to come right on in."

"I'm not sure where . . ."

"The first door down the hall, I gather," she said, lazily indicating the direction she meant.

"Thanks." Travers left her sitting there and went to the study door, rapping sharply on it. Galen's voice, muffled by the thick panel, called for him to come in.

He found Galen and Pritchard sitting on opposite sides of a desk in the small room, smoking cigars and talking in low voices. The walls were lined with shelves, and the shelves were filled with more books than Travers had ever seen in his life. The room was rather shadowy, its single window not admitting much light.

"Hello, Travers," Galen said. "We were just discussing you."

Travers nodded. He was having a hard time taking his eyes off the leather-bound spines of the books. He saw a few titles that he vaguely remembered from the few years he had spent in school, but most of them he had never heard of. "Have you read all these books?" he asked.

Galen smiled. "Not all of them, no. But most of them I have read. My father here early on instilled a love of the printed word in me. Do you read, Mr. Travers?"

"Never had much time for it," Travers replied. "Run across a few dime novels now and then, but that's about all."

Pritchard took a puff on his cigar, blew out the smoke. "Gaudy little pamphlets," he said. "Entertainment for the masses. Hardly the stuff of literature, eh?"

Galen smiled. "My father had a classical education, as you may be able to discern, Mr. Travers. I'm afraid it didn't give him quite the range of tolerance some of us have."

Pritchard snorted. "I just know what's good and what's not," he declared.

"Reckon I'm not going to argue that with either of you," Travers said. "What did you want to see me about, Mr. Pritchard?"

"First of all, just because you're going to be working for me doesn't mean that you can't call me Galen. I'd much prefer that."

"All right . . . Galen."

The rancher leaned forward and placed his cigar in a heavy glass ashtray. "I think we should discuss this Buckston problem." He waved Travers into another armchair. "What do you think we should do, Mr. Travers?"

"Well . . ." Travers settled back in the chair, balancing his hat on his knee. "Probably the best thing would've been to not buy that other spread in the first place. Buckston feels like you're pushing him, and it looks to me like maybe you are. Hope you don't mind me talking plain, Galen."

"That's exactly what I want you to do, Jacob. Or do you prefer Jake?"

Travers shook his head. "Jacob's fine. There's not much you can do now about buying the place, but you could offer to sell it to Buckston."

Galen sat back in his chair and put his cigar back in his mouth. "Never," he said flatly.

"Didn't figure you'd cotton to that idea. I suppose you could tell him you don't intend to run any stock on it. That might help matters."

"But I do intend to move my cattle onto that range. As I told you, I'm in the process of doing just that."

Travers met the rancher's level gaze and said, "Then you'd

better make sure your men always go armed, because sure as hell folks are going to be shooting at them."

Galen smiled. "That's where you come in, my friend. I should think with you and Mr. Moore on my payroll, Buckston would think twice about starting any more trouble. He certainly paid a high price for his villainy today."

Travers thought about the dead man and nodded. "Maybe so. But Buckston's liable to be willing to sacrifice a lot of men to hang on to what he believes is his. You don't know how these old-timers think, Galen. Once one of 'em goes on the prod, it's hard to stop things."

"Yes, well, Buckston is going to have to accept the fact that things have changed in this valley." Galen put the cigar in the ashtray again and clasped his hands together on the desktop. "I do appreciate your advice, Jacob; I don't want you thinking I don't. But here is what we're going to do. My riders are going to continue moving some of my herd onto the Demeter range. I want you and Emory Moore to accompany them to handle any trouble that might arise. Can I count on you for this, Jacob?"

Travers hesitated. He had told Galen Pritchard that he would ride for him, and that meant following the man's orders. It seemed like Galen was being unnecessarily stubborn about the whole thing, but legally, he had the right to use his range any way he saw fit.

"All right," Travers nodded.

"Excellent!" Galen stood up. "We'll show Buckston that he can't run roughshod over the whole territory any longer, eh? The man's long overdue for a comeuppance."

"Wouldn't know about that," Travers said. He stood up as well. "When do you want us to start moving cattle again?"

"Tomorrow is soon enough, I think. We're all a bit shaken from that dreadful experience this morning. And I need to pay a visit to La Junta this afternoon and conduct some business. Would you mind riding along with us, Jacob?"

"Sure."

Milburn Pritchard spoke up. "I believe I will accompany you

as well, my boy. There are a few supplies I would like to pick up for my wagon.''

Galen glanced over at him, a fleeting look of irritation passing over his face. ''I thought we had settled all that, Father. You're staying here on the ranch with me.''

''For the time being, yes,'' Pritchard replied. ''But I don't intend to be a permanent house guest.''

''Nonsense. Your place is here—''

Travers broke in to say, ''Excuse me, Galen, but if there's nothing else right now, I'll leave you and your pa to talk about this.'' He didn't want to intrude on what he considered family business.

''Certainly. We'll start into town right after lunch. I want Mr. Moore to stay here and keep an eye on the house while we're gone. Will you let him know?''

Travers nodded. He said, ''So long, Doc,'' to Pritchard, then left the study. When he passed through the living room on his way outside, there was no sign of Leanne Covington. She had probably gone to her room, he decided.

Emory grunted and nodded when Travers told him what Galen had said. ''I don't think Buckston will try anything else for a while,'' Emory said. ''Not after we made him and his men eat lead like we did this morning. But it won't hurt to keep a lookout.''

Lunch was uneventful. Everyone ate together, including the ranch crew, in the big dining room in the house. Travers saw that Leanne wasn't there, and when he got a chance, he asked Milburn Pritchard about her.

''The poor girl is indisposed,'' the Englishman replied. ''She's resting in her room. I'm afraid that frightful affair this morning has put her nerves in an awful state.''

''When I talked to her earlier, it looked like she'd been trying to calm them with some of that tonic of yours.''

Pritchard smiled. ''Isom's Elixir has great medicinal value, young man, but it is sometimes a bit potent for ladies with more delicate sensibilities. Dear Leanne may have indeed overindulged."

Travers bit back the angry response he felt to Pritchard's smugness. He was finding it harder and harder to like the old charlatan. If Leanne had been telling the truth in the stable, Pritchard had certainly taken advantage of her situation. He had taken a servant girl and turned her into his own private whore, and Travers didn't hold with that, regardless of the fact that Leanne seemed to accept it.

He didn't trust himself to say anything else to Pritchard, so he went back to the table and finished his meal. There was plenty of talk and laughter around the table. The hands were glad to be getting the rest of the day off, and they were also excited about the prospect of trouble with Buckston and his men. Cowboys were always eager for some sort of scrape, Travers had found, even when it meant risking their lives.

Travers heard Galen telling the Mexican woman Rosita to take a tray in to Miss Covington. When the meal was finished, Galen had a couple of the men hitch a team to the ranch's buckboard for the trip into La Junta. Travers was surprised when Leanne appeared in the living room wearing a tan skirt and jacket over a white blouse. There was a flat-crowned hat on her head, and she looked ready to travel.

"Rosita told me you're going into town, Doctor," she said to Pritchard. "Can I go with you?"

"Well, actually it's Galen who proposed the trip. I'm simply accompanying him."

"And it's fine with me if you come with us, Miss Covington," Galen put in as he entered the living room. "I'm sure you'll be the loveliest sight our little cattle town has seen in many months." He turned to Pritchard. "Do you think you could drive the buckboard, Father? I'll ride along on my mare."

"Certainly I can handle the buckboard," Pritchard snorted. "I've driven a wagon all over this bloody frontier, after all."

"Of course, Father," Galen said patiently. He glanced at Travers. "Are you ready, Jacob?"

"Whenever you are," Travers replied.

With a gallant flourish, Galen helped Leanne onto the seat of the buckboard, then mounted a fine-looking mare that one of the hands brought from the barn. Travers swung into the saddle of his horse and fell in on the other side of the wagon as Pritchard pointed it toward La Junta.

He got a better look at the ranch now as they followed the trail into town. The land was fine, rolling hills covered with plenty of graze as they sloped gradually toward the creek on the eastern boundary of the ranch. To the west, the hills rose, becoming more rugged until they turned into a range of small mountains. As Travers gazed to the north, he could follow the line of green that marked the creek's course. It ran past the town of La Junta, curving northwestward as it passed through Forrest Buckston's ranch. Somewhere up there, it angled into the hills and disappeared into the mountains where it was born in springs that would be clear and cold.

The ride into town would have been pleasant if Travers had been able to forget that they had been fighting for their lives earlier in the day and might have to do it again before they returned to the ranch.

La Junta was fairly busy for an afternoon in the middle of the week. Travers got his first good look at the settlement as they rode down the main street. The broad, dusty avenue was lined with businesses on both sides, and there were quite a few houses on the two cross streets. As cattle towns went, it wasn't overly large, but the residents of La Junta had a respectable little community here. Galen Pritchard directed his father to stop the buckboard in front of a large store whose sign proclaimed it to be Gilmore's Mercantile.

"I've ordered a few things from Mr. Gilmore," Galen explained, "and they should be in by now. I'm sure he can provide any supplies you need, Father, although I repeat it's not necessary for you to purchase a thing."

"I insist, my boy," Pritchard replied. "Come along, dear." He climbed down from the wagon and then gave Leanne a hand.

Travers hitched his horse at the rack in front of the store. He glanced across the street at a saloon called the Almarosa. A cold beer would have tasted good, but he thought he should stay with Galen and the others.

They went into the cluttered, high-ceilinged store. There were several customers already there being waited on by a couple of clerks. Travers had seen plenty of establishments just like it, gloomy, musty places full of just about all the odds and ends that anyone living on the frontier might ever need. Counters ran around all the walls, with more merchandise displayed under their glass tops.

A white-haired man was sitting at a desk behind the rear counter, but he got to his feet and hurried forward as soon as he spotted Galen. Extending his hand, he said, "Good day, Mr. Pritchard! How are you?"

"Just fine, Mr. Gilmore. Have those goods I ordered arrived yet?"

The merchant nodded. "I was going to send someone out to your ranch with word this afternoon, but you've saved me the trouble. Just got the shipment in this morning. I've got your order all ready for you, and I'll have one of the men carry it out and load it."

"Thank you. I appreciate your going to so much trouble for me, sir."

Gilmore smiled. "No trouble at all, Mr. Pritchard. Not for you."

Listening to the exchange, the message was clear to Travers. Galen Pritchard was on the verge of being a very important man around here. The storekeeper knew that Galen's ranch was growing, and he wanted to keep on the young Englishman's good side. Buckston's influence in these parts was clearly fading.

Which was probably one more reason Buckston was so proddy when it came to Galen and the UJ.

Galen turned to his father and said, "Mr. Gilmore, I'd like you to meet my father, Dr. Milburn Pritchard."

Gilmore effusively shook Pritchard's hand. "So very pleased

to meet you, sir. Your son has certainly been an excellent addition to our community."

"Indeed," Pritchard said, smiling. "Always knew the boy would go far."

"He definitely has." Gilmore turned his beaming face toward Leanne. "And who is this lovely young lady?"

"My, ah, assistant," Pritchard answered. "Miss Leanne Covington."

"Charmed, Miss Covington." And Gilmore obviously was, Travers thought as the merchant smiled at Leanne.

She nodded politely and said nothing for a moment. Then she suggested, "I wonder if I could look at some fabric, Mr. Gilmore. I believe I should make some new dresses."

Travers had been watching the doorway. He had looked over all the other customers when they came in and hadn't seen anyone who looked like a threat, so he had concentrated on the entrance to make sure Buckston or some of his men didn't taken them by surprise. Now a footstep on the planks of the floor made him glance over his shoulder, and a new voice said, "Perhaps I could help you, my dear. You must have a difficult time keeping up with the latest fashions."

The offer came from a young woman with blond hair who smiled sweetly at Leanne. The expression didn't extend to her eyes, though, which Travers saw were sharp and suspicious. The young woman was every bit as attractive as Leanne Covington, although she was much better dressed in a stylish silk gown. A feathered hat perched daintily on her mass of cornsilk curls.

"Why . . . thank you," Leanne said. "I wouldn't want to impose—"

"No imposition at all, my dear." The young woman moved her smile over to Galen Pritchard. "Galen, darling, you must introduce me to your new friends."

"Certainly, Rebecca," Galen replied. The look he exchanged with her implied friendship at least, if not something more. "Miss Rebecca Neely, this is my father, Dr. Milburn Pritchard, and his assistant, Miss Leanne Covington."

"Charmed, my dear," Pritchard said, taking Rebecca Neely's hand and pressing his lips to the back of it. A flush of satisfaction showed on Rebecca's beautiful face.

Leanne greeted her more coolly, her initial gratitude having lessened now. There was a mutual wariness as the two females shook hands.

"Rebecca's father is our local banker and a good friend of mine," Galen explained. "How is your father, my dear?"

"Why, he's just fine, Galen. And we're still expecting you for dinner tomorrow night."

Galen put his hand to his forehead. "It totally slipped my mind, dear. Thank you for reminding me."

Rebecca smiled again at Leanne. "And you shall certainly bring your father and your new friend with you, won't you?"

Pritchard said, "We would be honored, Miss Neely. Thank you for the invitation."

Leanne looked less enthusiastic, but she murmured her acceptance of the invitation. She had obviously not missed hearing the little endearments between Galen and Rebecca Neely.

Rebecca glanced at Travers, who was standing easy nearby with a hip propped on the top of a pickle barrel. To her, he was probably just another cowhand, and that was just fine as far as he was concerned. Something about Rebecca reminded him of Polly even more than Leanne did.

Rebecca looked away without asking for an introduction. Travers stayed where he was, one eye on the door. A grin tugged at his lips as he watched Leanne and Rebecca eyeing each other. Leanne had not shown any romantic interest in Galen Pritchard, but Rebecca's possessive attitude bothered her anyway.

The young blond woman looked like a good match for Galen. She would be the kind of wife an up-and-coming rancher needed . . . and her father was a banker.

"I'll see you tomorrow night, Galen," Rebecca said softly. She was more businesslike as she turned to Leanne and went on, "Now, dear, shall we find you some material for a decent dress?"

Leanne went with her to the other side of the store, although Travers saw sparks of anger dancing in the eyes of the black-haired girl.

Gilmore told one of his clerks to bring Mr. Pritchard's order from the back and load it onto his wagon. Travers moved forward and said, "I'd be glad to help."

"That's not your job, Jacob," Galen said.

"I know, but I don't mind."

Galen nodded. "In that case, go right ahead."

Travers waited until the clerk had dragged out several crates from the store's back room. Then he took one end of a box while the clerk took the other. Together, they carried it outside and slid it into the back of the buckboard. The word SHOVELS was written on the crate, and from the weight and the clanking of metal against metal, Travers believed it. The other crates, Travers saw as he and the clerk loaded them, contained more tools and construction equipment.

Galen must have some big project in mind, Travers thought.

The final crate, which was smaller than all the others, confirmed his guess. Each side of the box had CAUTION lettered on it in red, and a smaller legend announced that the box was full of dynamite.

Travers felt a nervous shiver go through him. He had never liked dynamite. Emory had used the stuff from time to time to blow bank vaults, but that had been before Travers joined up with him. He had heard the big man talking about it, though. There was something about knowing how much destructive power was contained in the box he was carrying that made Travers antsy, even though the stuff was supposed to be harmless until it was prepared for blasting.

He didn't know what Galen had in mind, but it had to be something important to make him order this much equipment. He had to have quite a bit of money sunk in this. No wonder he didn't want Buckston trying to hold him back.

Galen, Pritchard, and Gilmore came out on the store's porch as Travers finished loading the buckboard. Leanne emerged a moment later, carrying a bag full of cloth for her new dresses.

"Pritchard! Galen Pritchard!"

Travers turned quickly, thinking that someone might be calling Galen out. Instead he saw a tall, lean, middle-aged man hurrying down the sidewalk. The man wore a suit and a string tie, and there was a badge on his black coat.

Travers took a deep breath. A couple of years of dodging star packers made him want to cut and run. But the sheriff wasn't even looking in his direction. Instead, the lawman was frowning at Galen.

"Hello, Sheriff," Galen said as the man came up to him. "You appear to be rather agitated. What can I do for you?"

"Buck Buckston's been to see me," the sheriff replied curtly. "He said you killed one of his riders."

Galen's face tightened angrily. "Did he also tell you that he and his men shot up my house? If you'd like, you can ride out to the UJ with us and count the bullet marks in the walls."

The lawman shook his head. "Now don't get riled up, Pritchard. I'm just doin' my job and lookin' into a complaint."

"I'm the one who should be filing a complaint, Sheriff. Buckston seems to think he's the law in this valley."

"He found out you bought the Demeter place. That wasn't a smart move, son. You know how easy Buck gets his back up."

Galen snorted. "Well, he's going to have to get over that, isn't he? I did nothing illegal. The deal between Arthur Demeter and myself was completely aboveboard."

The sheriff rubbed his lean cheek. "Buck thinks you're movin' in on his range. Says when he went to talk to you about it, you cut loose at him with a rifle."

Galen shook his head. "I did no such."

"Well, somebody in your house did, then. Buckston swears that neither he nor any of his men fired the first shot."

"It's simple, Sheriff," Galen replied with a smile. "The man is lying."

Travers was glad Buckston wasn't around to hear that charge, or there would have been bullets flying right away. As it was, the sheriff was having a hard time holding in his anger.

"You're a respected man around these parts, Pritchard," he said, "but you don't know Buck Buckston. I've known the man for nigh onto thirty years, and he ain't a liar."

"Then he's mistaken. The incident this morning was rather hectic, after all."

The lawman shrugged thin shoulders. "Yeah, maybe. Guess it could've been that way. Some of Buck's riders are right proddy ol' boys sometimes." He pointed a finger at Galen. "But I still don't want a shootin' war in my county. You and Buckston settle this without guns, or I'll settle you!"

Galen made no reply, but his smile was faintly contemptuous.

After a moment, the sheriff said, "You just remember what I told you, Pritchard. The territorial governor's an old friend of mine. All I got to do is ask him and he'll see that federal troops are sent in. I won't have a range war."

"I'll remember, Sheriff," Galen said.

"See that you do." With that, the lawman turned and stalked off stiffly.

"Quite an unpleasant chap," Milburn Pritchard said, watching the sheriff's retreating back.

"Another of these old-timers who simply don't understand changing times," Galen said. "He'll see eventually that progress cannot be stopped. Delayed perhaps, but never stopped." He extended his arm to Leanne, all smiles again. "Well, my dear, shall we go? I expect you want to get some sewing done, now that you have that fabric."

"Yes. Thank you, Mr. Pritchard," she said. "I would have paid for my purchases, but Mr. Gilmore said you told him to put everything on your account."

"Indeed. I'm sure you'll be quite lovely in your new gown when we dine with the Neelys tomorrow night."

Leanne's face tightened at the mention of the upcoming dinner, but she rapidly smoothed out her expression as Galen helped her onto the buckboard. Travers mounted his horse and led the way as the little procession started back down La Junta's main street.

What he had learned this afternoon didn't ease his mind any. It looked to him like the town was choosing up sides. If the fight between Galen and Buckston spread to La Junta, the whole county could wind up spilling blood.

Travers was starting to wish he had ridden away this morning instead of turning around to answer the summons of gunfire.

Chapter Twelve

Travers began finding out the next morning—*early* the next morning—what it was like to be a cowhand.

The gray light of dawn was filtering into the bunkhouse when Emory Moore shook him awake. "Time to hit the trail, pard," Emory said, his voice disgustingly cheerful. "We have to earn our keep around here."

Travers sat up in the bunk, rubbing his eyes and pushing his hair back out of his face. "I'm awake, I'm awake," he muttered.

"Some of the boys are going to be pushing more stock up onto the old Demeter place today," Emory explained. "Galen wants us to go with them to make sure there's no trouble from Buckston's men."

Travers suppressed a groan. He had expected to be given chores like this, but he hadn't known they would begin so soon.

He climbed out of the bunk, staggered outside, and put his head under the cold stream that flowed from the pump. A couple of minutes of that made him start to feel human again.

Travers and Emory ate breakfast with the hands. Hotcakes,

bacon, and plenty of strong coffee made Travers feel even better. Galen Pritchard came into the big dining room before the meal was over, carrying a coffee cup in one hand and a sheaf of papers in the other. From the looks of things, he had been up for a while.

"Good morning, men," he said. He tossed the papers down on the table and took the seat at the head of it. "We're going to continue moving stock onto our new range today. Fred, I want you and five of the men to round up all the cattle you can find in the northwest canyon and start them toward the Demeter place."

The segundo nodded as he chewed a mouthful of food.

Galen turned his attention to the other side of the table. "The rest of you men go about your usual jobs," he said shortly.

There was no sign of Milburn Pritchard or Leanne this morning, and that didn't surprise Travers, either. No point in them being up this early.

Hell, it was the earliest he'd been up since before he left home.

As he went to the corral after breakfast to saddle his horse, he took in a deep lungful of the cool, clean morning air and saw the sun starting to creep over the eastern horizon. He wouldn't want a steady diet of rising at dawn, but every now and then it wasn't too bad, Travers thought.

His saddle was stowed in a corner of the barn. Travers went to pick it up. There were several other hands around, getting ready for the day's work, and Emory was strolling through the big double doors as Travers reached down to lift the saddle.

He saw the coiled shape under the saddle and heard the unmistakable warning buzz. Travers leaped back, dropping the saddle to the side, his hand flashing to his gun. "Rattler!" he yelled as he yanked the Colt from its holster.

The barn echoed with the blast of shots as he triggered the big revolver.

As he stared down at the bullet-shredded shape, Emory moved up beside him and said solemnly, "Yep, you sure blew hell out of that there lariat, Jacob."

Laughter beat against Travers's ears as the cowhands bunched around him. He took in the rolled-up piece of old rope with the rattlesnake rattles tied to one end of it. He saw the piece of twine that ran from the rattles to his saddle, attached so that it would make the rattles buzz when he lifted the saddle.

Travers disgustedly jammed his Colt back in its holster. "Damn you, Emory," he snapped. Then, after a moment, a grin started trying to tug at his mouth.

Emory slapped him on the back. "Just wanted to make you feel at home, son," he said.

"Don't worry about it, Travers," one of the hands told him. "This crazy pal of your'n's done worse than that to the rest of us. Some feller's goin' to shoot him over one of them jokes someday."

Travers grinned. He doubted that. Emory was too good with a gun to get shot over a practical joke.

The rest of the day wasn't particularly funny. It was, instead, plenty of hard work as Travers and Emory and the small group of punchers moved cattle. Travers and Emory might have been there primarily for protection of the other hands, but they did their share of the work. Taking his lead from Emory, Travers learned how to scare up wild-eyed cattle in the brush-choked canyon and head them toward the old Demeter place.

His initial impression of the new range had been correct, Travers saw that afternoon as they drove the stock north. As they moved onto the spread that Galen had bought from Demeter, Travers noted the rocky ground, the sparseness of the vegetation, the rough slopes of the foothills.

Arthur Demeter had probably been glad to unload the place, Travers thought. In the distance he could see one spot of green. When he pointed it out to Emory, the other man grunted, "That's where the creek comes out of the mountains. Runs across the corner of this range, then down through Buckston's place."

Travers nodded thoughtfully. He squinted his eyes and looked intently toward the area watered by the creek. He thought he saw a thin haze of dust in the air in that direction, but he couldn't be sure.

The work occupied them until late afternoon, and then Travers and Emory and the others started back toward the UJ. It was a good ride, but Travers discovered it didn't take nearly as long when they weren't having to drive a bunch of proddy cattle in front of them. The sun had almost disappeared behind the mountains to the west when the men rode up to the ranch headquarters.

Galen Pritchard was waiting for them at the bunkhouse. He listened intently to the segundo's report on the day's work, not saying anything until Fred was finished. Then Galen asked, "Any trouble?"

"No, sir, none at all."

"No sign of Buckston and his men?"

Fred shook his head.

Galen nodded in satisfaction and turned toward Travers. "Jacob, I'd like to see you in the house right away."

"Sure," Travers said. He swung down from the saddle and handed the reins of his horse to Emory. "Take care of him for me, will you?"

"You bet," Emory grinned. "I'll be right careful with that saddle of yours, too."

Travers shook his head and chuckled as he followed Galen toward the house. He was just asking for trouble, he knew, but maybe Emory had the mischief out of his system for a while.

Galen was waiting for him in the living room of the house. "Could I have Rosita bring you something to drink, Jacob?" he asked.

Travers shook his head. "No thanks. A beer'd cut the dust real good, but I reckon I'll wait until we've eaten."

"That's what I wanted to talk to you about. Remember that dinner invitation from Miss Neely?"

Travers frowned, a bad feeling suddenly popping up inside him. "I suppose I do," he said slowly.

"My father and Miss Covington and I will be leaving shortly to have dinner with Miss Neely and her father. I want you to come along with us, Jacob."

Travers started shaking his head. "I'm not much on fancy dinners, Galen," he began.

Galen held up a hand. "Don't worry. I don't want you to be uncomfortable." He grinned. "I know how men like you feel about suits and ties and such things. You can eat in the kitchen when we get there. But with all this trouble going on, I'd feel better if you rode along with us."

Travers sighed and then shrugged. Galen wasn't going to make a direct order out of this, he could tell, but the rancher seemed determined. Some men might have taken offense at his comment about eating in the kitchen, but Travers understood how he meant it. Galen honestly didn't want him feeling out of place, Travers sensed.

"Reckon if that's what you want," he said, "I can be ready to ride in just a few minutes. I'd like to wash up a little and put my saddle on a fresh horse. My big fella's about rode out after today."

Galen nodded. "Of course. We can leave in, say, fifteen minutes."

"That's fine."

As Travers started to leave the room, Galen said, "Don't worry, Jacob. I'm not really expecting any more trouble from Buckston just yet."

Travers nodded. He didn't explain that he wasn't very worried about Buckston either.

What was bothering him was the prospect of being under the same roof with Leanne Covington and Rebecca Neely. The way those two females had been sizing each other up the day before, Travers wouldn't be surprised if fireworks went off at this dinner.

Pritchard and Leanne didn't seem surprised that Travers was riding along with them to La Junta. Galen had probably told them earlier that he would be coming along.

Leanne was beautiful, Travers saw as she came out of the house and was helped aboard the buggy by Galen. She wore a light blue dress with a darker blue jacket over it, and her hair was piled up atop her head in an intricate arrangement of curls. Pritchard was wearing the same outfit he had been sporting when Travers first met him, right down to the swallowtail coat and top hat, the garments freshly cleaned now. Galen's dark suit was suitably sober for dinner with a banker.

For his part, Travers had donned a fresh shirt and knocked the dust off his hat and pants. Emory had had a few caustic comments to make about him dining with rich folks, but Travers had tried to ignore him.

Galen handled the team. Leanne sat beside him, while Pritchard took a position in the buggy's rear seat, leaning back and smiling expansively, obviously quite pleased to be accompanying his son tonight. He had to be proud of Galen, Travers thought. The young man had made quite a name for himself, judging by how folks around here treated him.

Darkness had fallen by the time they reached La Junta. Warm yellow light shone through the windows of the two-story house where Galen stopped the buggy. The house was the most impressive structure Travers had seen so far in La Junta, made of granite and looking more like a courthouse than a private residence. It was set behind a large lawn dotted with flower beds. A driveway curved through the lawn and led up to the house. A man was waiting at the front door to take the team once Galen had assisted Leanne down from the seat. Pritchard joined them, tugging down his coat.

Travers swung down from his horse. The hostler reached for the reins, but Travers said, "That's all right. I'll take care of him, if you'll just show me where."

Rebecca Neely appeared in the doorway of the house, resplendent in a low-cut, cream-colored gown. Behind her came a short, pudgy man wearing spectacles. There was a fringe of gray hair around his ears. Light from the lamp mounted on the wall beside the entrance shone on his bald head. He was smiling happily.

Rebecca stepped forward, her hands outstretched in greeting. Galen took them, leaned closer to her, and kissed her on the cheek. "So lovely to see you, my dear," he murmured. He released one of her hands to reach over and shake with the bald-headed man, who was evidently her father. "Thank you for the invitation, Thomas," Galen continued.

"You're quite welcome," the banker replied in a high-pitched voice. "I'm glad you could come, Galen." He looked past the rancher at Pritchard. "And this must be your father."

Galen performed the introductions all around. Thomas Neely shook hands with Pritchard and then bent to kiss the hand that Leanne offered him. "Charmed, my dear," he said.

Leanne tried to smile. She seemed a bit uncomfortable, and as Galen said, "Of course you and Leanne remember each other, Rebecca," the cause became evident.

"Of course," Rebecca said coolly. "My, what a lovely dress, Leanne. Such an improvement over what you were wearing yesterday."

Travers saw the spark flash in Leanne's eyes. Looked like his hunch was going to prove out. There was going to be trouble between those two.

But before he could see any more, the hostler said, "Come on, stable's out back." The man began leading the team around the house, and Travers fell in behind the buggy, bringing his horse with him.

Travers followed the man to a large stable behind the house, where he unsaddled the horse and put him in one of the empty stalls. He told the hostler, "Mr. Pritchard told me I could get something to eat in the kitchen. Been out on the range all day and didn't have a chance to sit down to supper before we rode over here."

The man nodded. "Sure thing. Just go in the back door and tell Maggie. She'll be glad to feed you." The man grinned in the light from the lantern just inside the stable door. "Watch yourself, though. Maggie's always got an eye out for good-lookin' young men."

Frowning at the warning, Travers headed toward the house. He spotted the back door, knocked once on it, and then entered.

He found himself in a large kitchen that was redolent with delicious aromas. A large ham sat on a cutting board with a knife beside it, and there was a big pan of biscuits on top of the massive iron stove.

No one was in sight.

Travers grinned and gave in to the urgings of his stomach. He snagged a couple of biscuits from the pan and then picked up the knife to carve off a hunk of the ham. It was juicy and hot and damned good, he found as he took a bite. And the biscuits were light enough to almost float out of his hand.

"What the devil are ye doin', lad?" a female voice suddenly asked behind him.

Travers turned around to see a redheaded woman almost as wide as the stove glaring at him. She wore a cotton dress and a billowing white apron, and she clutched a big spoon in her hand like a weapon.

With the smile still on his face, Travers said, "You must be Maggie."

"Aye, that I am. And who might you be, ya young scut?"

"Jacob Travers. I ride for Galen Pritchard. He wanted me to come along tonight and said I could get my supper out here in the kitchen."

Maggie sniffed. "The man's a mite free with his permissions, I'd say. But I never yet turned away a hungry man from my kitchen. I likes 'em to be well-fed 'fore they leave. So sit yourself down at that table, Jacob Travers. I'll be fixin' you a plate soon's I tend to the guests." A smile abruptly played across her broad features. "I could do with a mite o' company meself. I'm glad ye came."

Travers took a seat as instructed, dropped his hat on the floor beside him, and continued sampling the ham and biscuits as Maggie left the kitchen with a large tureen of soup. When she returned, true to her word, she prepared a plate of more ham, potatoes, and peas for Travers, setting it in front of him along with a bowl of the steaming soup and a heavy mug of equally hot coffee.

"I set a plain table, but good it is," she declared, and Travers had to agree with her. As he dug in, she sat down across from him and lowered her voice. "What would you be knowin' about that dark-haired lass with Mr. Pritchard?"

"Leanne?" Travers asked. "She's Dr. Pritchard's assistant."

"That'd be young Mr. Galen's father?"

"That's right," Travers nodded. "They've come to the UJ for a visit, but Galen's trying to talk them into staying."

Maggie's green eyes widened. "Ah, but that wouldn't set too well with Miss Rebecca, I'll be wagerin'. She's got her cap set for Mr. Galen her own self."

"I got that feeling," Travers said around a mouthful of ham. He sipped the strong coffee. He was well aware that he was gossiping with the stout Irish cook, but in a tense situation such as the one gripping this valley, there was no way of knowing what information might turn out to be important. "Rebecca intends to marry Galen, doesn't she?"

"Isn't that what I just said, man?"

"And with the backing of her father, the UJ might well grow into the biggest, most important spread in the territory." Travers's tone made it a statement, not a question.

"Mr. Galen's got his eye on the future, that's for sure," Maggie agreed. "He'd best keep growin', if he wants to keep Miss Rebecca interested."

Travers grinned again. "The little girl likes money and power, eh?"

He knew from the sudden frostiness in Maggie's eyes that he had gone too far. She could imply criticism of her mistress, but she didn't want any outsiders doing the same thing. Travers had gone beyond the bounds of proper gossip. Maggie pointed a blunt finger at his plate and said sharply, "Eat. There's pie when you're done."

She shoved her chair back and left the kitchen, heading for the dining room to see if there was anything else she could get for the guests.

Travers shook his head. He had learned a little bit about his employer tonight, and it didn't made him feel any better about the situation. Given Galen Pritchard's natural ambition and his interest in Rebecca Neely, there was no way he was going to ease off. He was going to keep pushing and pushing to grow until he and Buckston ran square into each other.

There had already been gunfire. Travers had a feeling there was going to be a lot more.

But, he shrugged, if there was any trouble tonight, at least he'd face it with a full stomach. Maggie was a damned good cook.

Travers reached for another biscuit.

Chapter Thirteen

Evidently there weren't any blowups during the meal. At least, Travers didn't hear anything unusual from the kitchen. During the ride back to the UJ, Galen and Leanne were quiet, saying little. Travers thought both of them seemed to have things on their minds.

Milburn Pritchard, on the other hand, had obviously had a fine time and put away a considerable amount of banker Neely's wine. "Fine chap for a moneylender, eh?" he said heartily.

"I like Thomas," Galen replied.

Pritchard leaned forward from the backseat of the buggy and laughed. "And that daughter of his is quite a beauty. You could do worse, Galen, much worse."

"Please, Father. Rebecca and I are just friends."

Pritchard nodded solemnly but sounded unconvinced as he said, "I'm sure that you are, my boy."

From his position riding beside the buggy, Travers couldn't see much of Leanne's face in the shadows, but he could tell that she was sitting up rather stiffly. Something was bothering her, and there was only one thing it could be.

She was interested in Galen Pritchard herself, and she was all too aware of how she compared to Rebecca Neely. It was highly unlikely that an enterprising young rancher would choose a penniless servant girl of dubious moral character over someone as beautiful and pure—and wealthy—as Rebecca.

Travers shook his head and turned his attention to the trail. He was glad it was their problem and not his. He'd always had enough trouble sorting out his own life, and every time romance had cropped up, it had only made things worse.

Still, he couldn't help but feel a pang of sympathy for Leanne. Her own background was something like his, full of things she couldn't be proud of, and yet some of it had been beyond her control.

He was trying to make a new start in life. There was no reason she shouldn't do the same.

When they passed the ranch, Travers dismounted while Galen was helping Leanne down from the buggy. Travers stepped over and said, "I'll take care of the buggy and the team."

"Thank you, Jacob," Galen said. "I trust the evening wasn't too unpleasant for you."

Travers thought about the double helpings of Maggie's food that he had put away. He smiled. "Nope. Not at all."

"Excellent. Good night, then."

Pritchard weaved slightly as he turned away from the buggy. "Yes, Mr. Travers," he said. "Good evening to you."

Travers nodded, then touched a finger to the brim of his hat as his eyes met Leanne's. Her skin was pale in the moonlight, and that made her eyes darker and more compelling, Travers discovered.

"Good night, ma'am," he murmured.

Leanne looked at him for a moment, then said softly, "Good night." She turned away on Galen's arm and allowed him to escort her through the gate and into the patio.

Holding his horse's reins in one hand and taking the harness of the buggy team's leader in the other, Travers started toward the barn. He had taken only a couple of steps when a figure materialized from the shadows.

"Any trouble?" Emory Moore asked, a rifle cradled in his arms.

Travers shook his head. "Not a bit. Not with Buckston, anyway."

"Something else happen?" Emory's mouth stretched into a grin. "That English gal and the banker's daughter get into a hair-pulling scrap?"

"No. But I don't think they like each other much."

"Miss Leanne can forget it if she thinks she can take the boss away from Rebecca Neely. She's a pretty enough gal, but she can't compete with what Rebecca's daddy's got. Not when Galen Pritchard wants to be the biggest man in this part of the country."

Travers glanced at Emory, then led the animals into the barn. "Help me get this team unhitched," he said. Then, after a moment, he went on, "Sometimes there's more important things than money and power."

Emory shook his head. His eyes shone in the glow from the lantern by the stable door. "Not to Galen Pritchard, boy. And not to me, either."

If Travers hadn't known better, he would have sworn over the next few days that there was no trouble in these parts. He and Emory and some of the other hands worked steadily moving stock onto the old Demeter place. Even though they rode close to Buckston's range several times, there was no sign of the proddy old rancher or his men. No one bothered the UJ hands as they went about their work.

Travers became more accustomed to the early hours and the hard labor, but he knew he would never get to like this way of life. For one thing, he had already been here a lot longer than he had intended. The urge to drift was still strong in him. But even though he liked Galen Pritchard a great deal less than he had first, Travers still felt like he was needed here.

He had seen Leanne several times around the ranch house but hadn't had the chance to say more than a dozen words to her. He would have liked to have known exactly what happened at that dinner at the Neelys', but to press her for the details would have been downright rude. From what he had seen of her cool behavior around Galen, though, he suspected that Leanne had given up any hopes she might have had for him.

For some reason, Travers discovered that he was glad of that.

Several days after the dinner in town, a carriage bearing Thomas Neely and Rebecca had drawn up one evening at the ranch. Neely and Galen had retreated into Galen's study, their faces serious, to discuss business. Dr. Milburn Pritchard had found himself left with the task of entertaining Rebecca, and he rose to the occasion gladly, regaling her with stories of life in England and yarns about his adventures in the West with the medicine wagon. Rebecca laughed merrily as Pritchard played the role of raconteur.

Travers noticed that Leanne stayed in her room during the whole visit.

Both Galen and Neely were smiling when they emerged from the study. They shook hands, and Neely said, "Whenever you're ready to proceed, Galen, just let me know. You know that you have my complete backing in this matter."

"Yes, indeed. And I appreciate it, Thomas."

Rebecca took Galen's arm. "Now, that's enough business talk for one night, you two. Galen, your father is such a dear! He tells the most wonderful stories."

Galen grinned. "Yes, Father is quite the storyteller, isn't he?"

Pritchard hooked his thumbs in his vest and sniffed. "Are you casting aspersions on my veracity?" he demanded.

"Of course not, Father. I'd never do that."

Travers was standing in the doorway between the living room and the dining room, lounging with his shoulder against the thick adobe wall. He had enjoyed listening to Pritchard's stories himself, even though he was sure that most of them were hogwash.

Now, to his surprise, Thomas Neely came over to him and said, "Good evening, Mr. Travers."

"Howdy," Travers nodded. What the devil did the bald-headed banker want with him?

"I wanted to tell you how glad I am you've decided to stay on here at the UJ. Galen is going to need all the good men he can get, and I'm sure you and Mr. Moore are two of the best."

Galen came over quickly as Travers began to frown. "Jacob knows how important he is around here, Thomas," he said. "Any ranch needs all the good hands it can get."

Travers knew damn well he was no great shakes as a cowhand and never would be. Galen knew it, too.

What Neely was saying, Travers suddenly realized, was that before too much longer, Galen was going to need gunmen. Men like him—and Emory Moore.

Galen steered Neely away, concealing his irritation behind a big smile. Travers could see it, though, and knew that Galen was unhappy with the banker. Neely had been implying that more violence was about to break, and it had to have something to do with whatever they had been discussing inside the study.

Travers slipped out through the dining room, leaving their laughter behind him, and headed for the back door. When he was outside in the clear night air, he strolled toward the bunkhouse. Somehow his fingers strayed down to the butt of his gun and played lightly over the walnut grips.

"Don't be a damned fool," Travers muttered to himself. "Get on your horse and get out of here now, while you've got the chance."

But he knew he wouldn't.

"Watch those cattle!" one of the hands yelled. "Travers, that bunch is breaking off!"

Travers blinked dust out of his eyes and called, "I see 'em!" He spurred his horse into a faster gait, trying to cut off the small jag of cattle that were veering off from the main bunch. Behind him, Emory picked up the pace of his own mount.

A few more days had passed, and so far there had still been no trouble. Travers and Emory accompanied Galen's hands every day as they pushed more stock onto the Demeter range, but Buckston and his men were nowhere to be seen.

The waiting had Travers's nerves drawn taut.

Something was going to happen sooner or later, and sooner was all right with him.

He and Emory pulled their weight, and it wasn't unusual for them to go after some proddy steers like they were doing now. As Travers rode easily in the saddle, he reflected that this job was going to have to come to an end soon. Even his untrained eye could see that this arid range wasn't going to support many more beeves than what had already been moved onto it.

The handful of cattle he was chasing darted around a clump of mesquite at the mouth of a dry wash. The slope leading into the arroyo was gentle, and the cattle thundered down it, raising more dust.

Travers grimaced and pulled the bandanna around his neck up over his nose in an effort to keep out some of the dust. He ducked his head slightly as he adjusted the cloth.

A slug whined by his ear.

Instinct took over. Travers ducked lower and heeled his horse into a gallop. He heard another bullet zip past his head, not as close this time. The crack of a rifle came faintly to his ears.

Hooves pounding, Emory's horse pulled up next to Travers. "Somebody's shootin' at us!" Emory yelled.

Travers nodded grimly. Their mounts plunged down the slope into the arroyo. The banks of the wash might give them a little more cover, but they could also represent a trap. Travers slipped his Colt from its holster and squinted against the dust, trying to locate whoever was shooting at them.

When they were both in the arroyo, Travers hauled back on the reins and pulled his horse to a stop. The fleeing cattle were forgotten now. Emory halted, too, his eyes scanning one direction while Travers checked the other way.

"See anything?" Emory asked tensely.

Travers peered through the settling dust. "Not a damn thing," he replied. "I don't hear any more shots, though."

"They probably can't see us down here."

"What do you think we should do?"

Emory hesitated a moment before answering, then said, "Maybe we should split up."

He wants to run out on me again. The thought went through Travers's mind before he could stop it. He had been able to work with Emory and keep things polite enough, but he would never forget the way the man had left him behind to die in Grady.

But maybe this time Emory had a point.

"They're probably covering the arroyo," Travers said. "If we come up out of it at two different places, chances are they won't be able to get both of us."

"And then we can spot where they're firing from."

Travers nodded. "All right. Let's do it."

He wheeled his horse and galloped down the sandy bed of the wash. Behind him, he heard Emory riding away in the other direction.

Travers holstered the Colt and pulled his Winchester from its saddle boot. He wasn't as good with a long gun as he was with the pistol, but there was a good chance Buckston's men were out of the Colt's range.

The arroyo curved toward the foothills. Travers followed it for at least half a mile. There had been no more shots since he and Emory entered the wash, but he was willing to bet that somewhere at least one man had a rifle pointed in this direction.

Travers angled his horse toward the side of the arroyo. The banks were steeper here, but he spotted a place that looked gradual enough for his mount to negotiate. Travers levered a shell into the Winchester's chamber as he started up the slope.

He had the horse running as it emerged from the wash. Travers steeled himself for the impact of a bullet that didn't come. He heard the blast of a rifle, but it was nowhere close to him.

It came from back down the arroyo . . . back where Emory had ridden.

Travers wheeled his horse as the sound of another shot came drifting to him. His narrowed eyes searched the foothills, seeking the bushwhacker's position.

Suddenly he heard hoofbeats and looked over his shoulder. Three riders had come into view, and as they spotted him, they let out whoops and started toward him at a gallop. He saw puffs of smoke and heard the brittle crackle of pistol shots.

More of Buckston's men, Travers thought. He yanked his horse around and snapped the Winchester to his shoulder. The range was pretty far for handguns, so the rifle would help him even the odds. He pressed the trigger.

The slug kicked up dust twenty yards in front of the three men. Travers jacked the lever and fired again, this bullet going into the ground even closer to the oncoming riders. They slowed momentarily.

Travers kicked his horse into a gallop.

He headed for the rugged foothills, angling northwest. That course didn't take him directly away from his pursuers, but he thought it offered the best chance to lose them. They probably knew the country better than he did, but he was one man on a good horse. He would give them the slip if at all possible.

Odds of three against one were too steep. He'd faced long odds before, but he wanted to avoid this trap if he could.

He slid the Winchester back in its boot and looked back. The riders hadn't gained any on him, but they had broken out their own rifles. He wasn't too worried about any of them hitting him, not when they were firing from galloping horses.

As the terrain became rougher, Travers's mount took it in stride. He rode around some hills, over others, and finally ducked back into another dry wash while he was momentarily out of sight of his pursuers.

No, he realized, it wasn't a different arroyo. It was the same one he had ridden through earlier. Its curving course had brought him back to it. He was riding almost due west now as he followed the wash through the foothills. The hills were turning into mountains, looming higher and higher above him.

Travers slowed his horse to a trot and watched his back trail. There was no sign of the three men who had been chasing him. He took a deep breath. It looked like he might have lost them.

He stayed in the arroyo, following it deeper into the mountains. He was still on the range that Galen Pritchard had bought from Demeter, but he would be reaching the boundary soon. When he found a likely looking spot, he rode up the bank and came out onto a high, tree-dotted bench.

There was grass here, and the trees looked healthy enough. Travers looked back the way he had come, the land falling away so that he could gaze out over the whole valley. He saw the winding strip of green that led from this bench down into the valley and knew that the springs which fed La Junta Creek had to be close by.

Here and there, cattle grazed, but Travers saw no riders. He sighed in relief again. The ambush had failed.

At least as far as he was concerned, it had. He had no idea what had become of Emory Moore. There had definitely been some shooting back in that direction. . . .

He would head back to the UJ, Travers decided. Emory would do the same if he had gotten away from the bushwhackers.

But before doing that, Travers decided to give in to his curiosity. He had thought when he arrived in this part of the territory that someday he would find the head of the creek and drink from its waters. He was closer to it now than he had ever been.

He turned the horse toward the mountains again.

Travers rode across the benchland. The arroyo was still in sight to his left. It probably wasn't a typical dry wash, cut by runoff from the rains in the mountains, but rather an actual streambed. Travers mused on that. At one time, far in the past, La Junta Creek had probably flowed between its banks, until some unknown event had altered its course. Avalanche, earthquake, who knew what had caused the change?

A half hour later, Travers found the springs.

He halted his horse and stared in consternation at what he saw. The arroyo was close at hand. He rode slowly over to it and looked at the obviously man-made embankments that had lengthened the wash until it nearly reached the crystal pool where the creek bubbled out of the side of a hill. The stream was small here as it led away from the pool, a narrow trickle that would grow as it flowed through a narrow cut and then out of the foothills, bringing life to the valley.

No one was around at the moment, but it was clear that men had been working frequently here. With narrowed eyes, Travers looked from the creek to the springs to the arroyo, and a terrible suspicion sprang full-blown into his mind.

Damn Galen Pritchard!

The dynamite and the construction equipment the rancher had ordered made sense now. Travers was looking at the reason. Once the wash was extended just a little farther, one dynamite blast could close off the cut where the creek now flowed. The water would have nowhere else to go except down the arroyo.

Down the arroyo through the Demeter place and on through the center of the UJ. With one blast, Galen Pritchard would have the valley's water completely under his control.

Buckston would be ruined, and so would all the other, smaller spreads. Galen would have what he wanted then, the biggest, best ranch in this part of the territory.

And Travers knew with a horrible certainty that Galen Pritchard wouldn't give a damn what his actions meant to anyone else.

The crack of a rifle cut through Travers's reverie.

He spun in the saddle and spotted the three riders racing toward him. He hadn't lost them after all.

Grimacing, he pointed his horse's head toward the springs and yelled as it took off with a spurt of speed. The animal thundered past the pool. Just up the slope of the hill, a deadfall caught Travers's eye. Several trees were down, and their trunks formed a natural fortification.

Travers veered toward the fallen trees and left the saddle in a dive as he jerked his own Winchester loose. He hit hard and had to gasp for breath for a second. Bullets chewed splinters from the thick trunks above his head.

He came up on his knees and rested the rifle on the logs. Buckston's men were close enough now that he could make out their faces. He recognized all three of them from his first run-in with the old rancher, when the puncher called Hewett had almost been strung up.

Travers didn't want to kill them.

He knew now what Galen was up to, and a sick feeling in the pit of his stomach told him he had been on the wrong side all along.

Travers fired twice.

His first bullet sang close by the head of one of the men. The second took off another man's hat, sending it spinning away. Travers grimaced. He hadn't intended to come that close with either shot.

But it did the trick. Buckston's men must have suddenly realized they were charging a well-armed man behind good cover, a man who was experienced with guns. They yanked their horses to a stop and then turned them around.

Travers had to grin as he watched the men ride frantically back in the direction they had come. He could have dropped all three of them, more than likely, but he let them go. They had gotten caught up in the excitement of the chase, and no doubt they were now good and scared as they realized how close they had come to getting killed.

Travers hoped they weren't just regrouping for another try. He watched, waiting behind the deadfall until they were out of sight. Then he stood up, his side aching from the fall he had taken. His horse was close by, grazing calmly now that the shooting was over. Travers's hat had come off when he dove out of the saddle, and he bent to pick it up before retrieving the animal.

He stopped short, bending over with one hand on his hat. From this position, he got a better look at the ground underneath the fallen trees.

It looked like someone had been digging there recently.

Travers studied the trees themselves. They hadn't been toppled for very long; he could tell that by the dried leaves that were still clinging to some of the branches. As he straightened and settled his hat on his head, he walked over to the base of the trunks.

He had figured that wind had blown the trees down, but now he saw differently. From the looks of the damage, something else had happened.

Like dynamite, maybe?

Travers frowned. He had been sticking his nose into other people's business for weeks now, and all it had brought him was trouble. But he suddenly realized he had to know why someone had blown these trees down on top of some dug-up ground.

He thought he already knew the reason.

He worked quickly, using his horse and rope to pull the trees far enough to one side so that he could start digging. The small folding shovel that he carried in his saddlebags, like all the other hands, wasn't much good for this job, but Travers stayed with it as the sun began to get low in the sky. He was afraid he was going to run out of light.

Dusk was settling down over the hills when he finally reached the body. Travers's jaw was set in a tight, grim line as he brushed dirt away from the man's face.

He'd never seen the dead man before, at least not that he could remember. The man had been dead for several weeks, so Travers couldn't be sure. He looked over the body, searching for something he could use to make some sort of identification.

The last two fingers of the man's left hand were missing. It wasn't much, but maybe it would be enough.

Travers stood up. For the final time, he considered riding on over these mountains, out of this country where nothing was what it seemed.

Then he began filling in the grave once again. He'd leave the body here for the time being.

When he was through, he had a lot of riding to do.

And a lot of questions to ask.

Chapter Fourteen

It was dark when Travers reached La Junta. The general store was still open, and of course the saloons were going strong, but other than that, the town appeared to be closed for the night. Travers rode past Gilmore's place and found the sheriff's office several doors up the street.

A light was burning in the window of the little adobe building. Travers hitched his tired horse to the rail in front of the office, stepped up onto the sidewalk, and opened the door.

The middle-aged lawman looked up from his desk. He was eating his supper from a tray in front of him. He looked at Travers in vague recognition and said, "What can I do for you, son?"

Travers took a deep breath. Just being in a sheriff's office made him nervous. This one looked too much like the one back home, from the paper-littered desk to the gun racks on the walls to the cell block in the rear which he saw through an open door with a barred window in it.

"You mind if I ask you a few questions, Sheriff?" he asked.

The lawman shrugged. "I suppose not. Don't I know you?"

"I ride for Galen Pritchard," Travers said without offering his name.

The sheriff nodded. "That's right. I remember seeing you down at Gilmore's with Pritchard awhile back. Pritchard had his pa with him."

"That's right." Travers didn't want to talk too much about himself. Quickly, he went on, "Sheriff, you knew that Demeter fella, didn't you?"

"Art Demeter? Sure, I knew him." The sheriff picked up his coffee cup and sipped from it as he regarded Travers curiously.

"What happened to him after he sold his place to Pritchard?"

"Well, I don't rightly know. I don't think I saw him after that. Pritchard brought all the paperwork into town and got the sale recorded and the deed changed over. I seem to recall he said that Demeter planned to move on, to California, maybe. He didn't have any family around here, nothing to keep him."

That bad feeling was rolling around in Travers's stomach again. All during the ride to La Junta, he had hoped that his suspicions were wrong.

"So it's possible nobody around here saw Demeter after he sold his ranch to Pritchard?"

The sheriff nodded. "I reckon that's so."

Travers held up his left hand and bent the last two fingers down. "Was Demeter missing some fingers, like this?"

"Sure. He got careless roping a steer when he was just a youngster, he always said. Got those fingers caught when he tried to tie off the rope. Took 'em right off when that steer's weight hit the rope." The sheriff frowned and pushed his meal tray away. "Now I've answered some questions for you, mister. Answer some for me. What's all this to you?"

Travers shook his head. He had been expecting what the sheriff had told him, even though he had hoped for some other explanation. He said easily, "I just got to thinking that maybe I used to know the man. The Demeter I knew had two fingers gone, all right. I thought if he was still around here, I'd look him up."

The sheriff leaned back in his chair. "Oh." He scratched one sideburn. "Well, that makes sense, all right. Damn, you really had me curious for a minute. Couldn't figure out why one of Pritchard's riders would be asking such questions. Demeter had already sold his land and moved on before you got here, hadn't he?"

"Yeah, I guess so." Travers was ready to get out of here now. He hoped that his explanation had really satisfied the sheriff.

"It was that other fella, that Emory Moore, who signed on with Pritchard just before his deal with Demeter. I was getting the two of you mixed up."

Travers nodded. "Well, thanks, Sheriff. I didn't want to say hello to Demeter enough to go chasing after him." He went to the door, said good night, and left the lawman to finish his meal.

Travers jerked the reins loose and swung up into the saddle. He rode quickly out of town, headed for the UJ.

The buggy belonging to Thomas Neely was parked in front of the house when Travers got there. Travers wasn't sure which one was more tired, him or his horse. Chances were the day's work wasn't over for either of them.

He tied the horse to the rail next to the buggy's team and went through the gate into the patio. The lantern that hung next to the big front door was lit, casting its glow over the courtyard. Travers wondered what Neely was doing here. He wasn't surprised by the banker's visit, though. Considering that Neely was probably Galen's partner in the scheme to divert the creek, there were plenty of reasons for him to be around the ranch house.

But as Travers opened the front door and stepped into the house, he saw that his assumption had been wrong. Thomas Neely had not come out to the ranch in the rig tied up outside.

Rebecca had.

She and Galen were on the long sofa, wrapped up in each other's arms. Galen took his mouth away from Rebecca's as Travers's boots thumped on the planks of the floor. He looked up, a smile on his face.

The smile dropped away as he saw the grim expression that

Travers wore. "What is it, Jacob?" he asked quickly, straightening up. Rebecca calmly did the same, seemingly not embarrassed at all by the intrusion.

"Emory get back here all right?" Travers asked.

"Why, no, I don't believe he's returned. The hands said that you and he got separated from them. I assumed that the two of you were together."

"Didn't they tell you about the shooting?" The other hands had to have heard the gunfire that afternoon.

"They did say something about it. Did you run into some of Buckston's men?"

Travers pushed his hat to the back of his head. "You don't seem very worried about that possibility."

Rebecca stood up and moved unhurriedly away from the sofa. Galen got to his feet as well. "Of course I was concerned. But I have every confidence in you and Emory. I know you can handle anything you might run into."

Travers took a deep breath. He wanted to clench a fist and smash it into Galen's handsome face, but instead he said, "There was some trouble. Emory and I had to split up. Some of Buckston's men chased me up into the foothills, to the springs where the creek starts."

A change came over Galen's features. "I see. And now you're wondering just what's being done up there."

Travers shook his head and said, "I'm not wondering about a damned thing. I know you're about to change the course of the creek."

Rebecca had paused beside the fireplace, cold now at this time of year. She placed her hands behind her and leaned against one of the thick timbers supporting the mantle. "And what's wrong with that?" she asked.

Travers glanced at her. "You knew about it, ma'am?"

"Of course. Galen and I plan to be married, Mr. Travers. We have no secrets from each other."

Travers looked into her blue eyes. "Then you know that your future husband is a murderer?"

Breath hissed sharply between Galen's teeth. He took a step forward, his hands fisting at his sides.

He stopped short as he found himself looking down the barrel of Travers's Colt.

"Just stand still," Travers said flatly. "I know all about it, Pritchard. I know how you forced Demeter to sign the papers giving you his range, then killed him so that he couldn't back out of the deal. You planned all along to divert the creek once you had the springs under your control."

Galen stared wide-eyed at him, and Rebecca looked equally astounded. "You're insane!" Galen snapped. "I've killed no one. I don't deny that I intend to alter the course of the stream, but that's my business. It's on my land."

"Land you got by killing Demeter," Travers grated.

Galen shook his head. "I swear to you, Travers, I don't know what you're talking about. It's true I had a bit of trouble finalizing the sale with Demeter, but it was all legal and aboveboard. I paid him cash, and he moved on."

"What kind of trouble?"

Galen flushed angrily. "We agreed to terms, and then at the last minute Demeter decided he wanted more money. Well, I'll tell you, Jacob, I'm not the sort of man to put up with that. I sent Emory over there with the contracts and the money and a message—"

Galen broke off suddenly, catching his breath. Travers felt the same shock of understanding. Slowly, he said, "Emory went over to the Demeter place? Alone?"

Galen didn't answer for a moment. Finally, he said, "Yes. Alone."

"You trusted a new man with a job like that, carrying enough cash to buy a ranch?"

"Emory knew I was having a difficult time with Demeter," Galen said. His face had gone pale. "I knew it was a risk, but when he volunteered to persuade Demeter to accept our original terms, I . . . I allowed him to do so."

Travers took a deep breath. He was beginning to understand.

In some part of his brain, Galen had known there was a good chance Emory would rough up Demeter, if that was what it took to get him to sign the papers. Then Emory could kill Demeter and keep the cash as payment for doing the job. Galen had been willing to lose the money to have clean hands and a signed contract. Then he could go ahead with his plans, maybe even convincing himself that he was just an honest businessman trying to improve his holdings.

Rebecca Neely stepped forward and took Galen's arm. "Don't listen to him, darling," she said urgently. "He's just some drifter who doesn't know what he's talking about. You can't let him ruin all of our plans."

Galen looked over at her, saw the pleading in her eyes as plainly as Travers did. But, Travers wondered, did Galen see the greed there as well? Rebecca knew damn well what had happened to Demeter now, knew it just like he and Galen did.

Galen took a deep breath. He said, "Rebecca's right, Jacob. You're being foolish. Now put that gun up. If you leave right now, we'll say no more about any of this."

Rebecca's fingers tightened on his arm. "No, Galen. I think Mr. Travers should leave the ranch."

A smile with no humor in it played across Travers's face. "Your lady doesn't want me around as a reminder, Galen," he said. He slid the Colt back in its holster. "And I don't reckon I want to stay around here, either. But you'd best think twice about what you're planning to do with that creek."

"It's my land," Galen said stubbornly.

"But if you go through with it, you'll ruin everybody else in the valley. Maybe it won't be illegal, but it'll sure as hell be wrong."

Galen laughed shortly. "You're a fine one to talk about that. You're a gunman, Travers. I should think you're hardly the man to be giving a lecture on morals."

Travers swallowed. He had thought that same thing himself, more than once today. But he couldn't shake the memory of old George back at Ghost River. A man can't help what he's been,

George had said, but he can sure as hell do something about what he's going to be.

"I won't let you do it, Galen," he said softly.

"You can't stop us," Rebecca spat at him, anger contorting her lovely face and making it ugly. Contemptuously, she went on, "What are you going to do?"

For a long moment, Travers stared at the two of them.

And then he said, defeat plain in his voice, "Don't reckon there's anything I can do."

"That's right," Galen said. "Get your gear and get off my land, Travers. When Emory gets back, I intend to tell him that you're not welcome here any longer."

"In other words, you'll set your hired killer on me."

Galen's face darkened in fury. "Get out!"

"I'm going." Travers wheeled and stalked out of the room.

He didn't leave by the front door, however. He went down the hall, ignoring Galen and Rebecca. He had a feeling that Leanne Covington was in her room, and when he rapped on the door, her voice came from inside. "Who is it?"

"Travers," he said. "I've got to talk to you."

Her door opened a moment later. She looked out at him curiously, holding a dressing gown closed at her throat. "What is it?" she asked. "Is something wrong?"

"Everything." He glanced down the hall toward the living room. There wasn't much time. Galen would get over being angry soon and start to think. Once he did, he would know damn well that Travers had given up too easily.

"I don't understand—"

Travers reached out, took her wrist, and gently tugged her into the hall. "Come with me," he said.

Leanne started to protest, but something about his face silenced her. She came with him as he left the house through the back door and circled around toward the bunkhouse.

"Wait here until I get my traps," he told her, leaving her in a patch of shadow.

He hoped she would do as he asked. For some reason, it was

important to him that she know what was happening.

He went into the bunkhouse. The hands swarmed around him, wanting to know what had gone on that afternoon. Travers answered them curtly, telling them that he and Emory had run into some of Buckston's men who wanted to trade lead. As he talked, he gathered his gear.

Fred, the segundo, caught his arm. "You pulling out?" he demanded.

"That's right."

"What about the time you've got coming?"

Travers shook his head. "It's not enough to make me stay here," he said. Besides, he added to himself, he had just been fired.

Draping his warbag over his shoulder, he turned to the door. The other hands stared after him, baffled by this unexpected turn of events. Travers wasn't in the mood to offer any more explanations.

There was only one person he wanted to talk to now.

Leanne was waiting for him where he had left her. As he stepped up to her in the darkness, she gasped and reached out to clutch his sleeve. "Oh!" she said. "It's you. You frightened me, Mr. Travers."

He wanted her to call him Jacob, but there was no time to talk about that now, either. "Listen," he said. "There's going to be a lot of trouble around here. If you can leave, I think you should."

"Trouble? What kind of trouble?"

Travers took a deep breath and launched into the story. He told it as quickly and simply as he could, breaking it down to the bare facts he knew and the ones he had figured out. Leanne's hand gripped his arm tighter and tighter as he talked.

When he was done, she shook her head and said, "No. No, I can't believe it."

"It's true," Travers assured her.

"What you said about Emory Moore . . . about him killing that other rancher . . . I can believe that. I saw him shoot one of the

Buckston men in the back during that fight here at the ranch."

"Emory did that?" Somehow Travers wasn't surprised.

"Yes. And he started it by firing the first shot. I saw him do that, too. But I can't believe that Galen . . . that Galen would have anything to do with such things. He wouldn't harm anyone."

Coldly, Travers said, "He'd step on anyone who got in his path, Leanne, and Rebecca Neely will be pushing him every inch of the way. He may not have told Emory to kill Demeter, but he knew that's how it would probably turn out. And he'll be ruining every other rancher in this valley if he goes through with his plans for the creek. That's why I've got to stop him."

"But what can you do?" Leanne asked, unconsciously echoing Rebecca's question.

"Tell Buckston."

"But if you do, he'll fight. . . ."

Travers nodded. "It'll mean war, all right. No getting around it."

The words were barely out of his mouth when he heard the soft step behind him. He spun, reaching out with one hand to thrust Leanne against the wall of the house, out of the line of fire. His other hand went to the Colt on his hip, drawing it smoothly and earing back the hammer.

Milburn Pritchard stepped into a patch of moonlight, holding his hands up, palms out, to show that he was unarmed. The doctor's teeth were bared in a grimace, and his bearded face was set in bleak lines.

"Don't shoot, Mr. Travers," he said quickly. "It is only me."

Travers drew a deep breath. "Dammit, Doc, sneaking up on a man like that's a good way to get shot."

"I'm sorry. But I overheard what you've been telling this poor girl, and I have no other option except to say that you are an unmitigated liar, sir!"

Travers laughed harshly. "You think it's a lie, Doc, you just wait and see what your son does. I know you don't want to think bad about Galen, but I reckon he's changed since he came over here."

Pritchard shook his head. "No. I don't know why you want to spread such malicious lies about my son, but I simply cannot allow it." He stepped closer, doubling his fists. "If you insist on going to that man Buckston, I shall have no choice but to thrash you, Mr. Travers."

Travers saw the determination on Pritchard's face. The old man was a pompous, lecherous windbag, but at the moment he was a father defending his child, and that made all the difference in the world.

Slowly, Travers said, "Just back off, Doctor. I don't like everything you've done, but I don't want to hurt you."

Pritchard held out a hand. "Come to me, Leanne."

Travers glanced at the girl. She was looking back and forth between him and Pritchard, obviously torn by her emotions. He sensed that she wanted to believe what he had told her.

There was no point in making things harder on her. He couldn't take her with him now anyway. "Go on," he said softly to her. "Just be careful."

She nodded, stepped over to Pritchard, and then moved past him, head down, hurrying toward the back door of the house. Travers watched her for a moment, then switched his attention back to Pritchard.

"Now, Doc," he said reasonably, "you'd better go with her."

"No, sir. Not until I have your word that you won't go to this Buckston ruffian and cause more trouble for Galen."

Travers sighed. "You don't understand. I've got to tell him what Galen intends to do—"

"In that case, sir, have at you!"

The punch that Pritchard threw at him was slow. Travers moved his head to the side and avoided it easily. He fended off several more wild blows. Pritchard was puffing and blowing from the exertion within seconds.

The doctor was going to hurt himself if Travers didn't put a stop to this. He blocked another punch, measured the older man with his eyes, and then clipped him on the jaw with a short right. Pritchard staggered back a step and then sat down hard on the ground.

"Sorry, Doc," Travers said.

Pritchard let out a moan and lifted a hand to rub his sore jaw. Travers shook his head and turned toward his horse. He mounted quickly and walked the animal back over to where Pritchard was still sitting in the dirt.

"Wish it had worked out different," Travers said, and meant it.

He rode away from the ranch at a hard gallop.

Chapter Fifteen

Travers figured he was about halfway to Buckston's ranch when the bullet came out of the darkness, clipped his left shoulder, and knocked him out of the saddle.

The fall knocked the wind out of him, but he had the presence of mind to roll rapidly to one side as he grabbed for his Colt. His shoulder was numb right now, not hurting yet, but he knew that would come later.

He came up onto his feet, running for a stand of small trees fifty feet away. The rifle cracked again in the night, and this time the slug thudded into the ground just behind him. Out of the corner of his eye, Travers saw the muzzle flash and snapped a shot in that direction.

Another bullet whapped by his head as he ducked into the trees. Travers crouched behind one of the narrow trunks and lifted his pistol. The trees didn't provide much cover, but they were better than nothing. He triggered twice at the spot where the ambusher had been and then dodged behind another tree.

That didn't mean the man was still there, however. He was

smart enough to do some moving around himself. The rifle blasted a few feet away from where it had been. Travers jerked a shot that way.

There was still one bullet left in the Colt, but he took advantage of the opportunity to reload anyway. He thumbed five fresh cartridges into the gun, not leaving the hammer on an empty chamber this time. He might need all six shots to get out of this mess.

Travers reached up and touched the wetness that was spreading on his shirt. His shoulder was starting to hurt a little. Soon, he knew, it would be on fire. His arm moved well enough, so he hoped that no bones were broken. From the feel of it, he was just creased.

It was still going to hurt like hell in a little while.

He cast his eyes around, trying to locate his horse. He spotted the animal waiting nervously on the other side of the clearing. That was where the bushwhacker was. Travers grimaced. He couldn't afford to lose his horse.

A slight rustle of brush came from across the clearing. Travers yanked the Colt's barrel over and started to fire, holding off at the last instant. The bastard was probably just trying to draw his fire and get him located.

Travers felt around on the ground with his left hand and found a good-sized stick. He tossed it to the side, creating his own diversion. He crouched, ready to fire if the other man bit.

Silence from the other side of the clearing.

A grim smile played across Travers's lips. Maybe they could sit here all night, throwing sticks and waiting. The sheer ridiculousness of the situation struck him as funny.

But that didn't make it any less dangerous.

The horse broke the stalemate. The bushwhacker must have tried to sneak up and grab the dangling reins, because the animal suddenly whinnied and shied away.

Travers fired instinctively, blasting three shots into the clump of brush next to the horse. One of the slugs ricocheted off something with a vicious whine, and then Travers heard a grunt of pain. There was a crashing in the brush. Travers fired once more at the sound.

Then, as he held his fire for a moment, he heard the creak of saddle leather and the sudden beat of hooves. The ambusher had had his own horse tied up over there, and now he was making his escape.

Travers waited a few minutes, just to be sure it wasn't some kind of trick, then stood up and moved into the clearing. His insides were jumping around as he moved into the moonlight, but no shots came at him. The other man seemed to be gone.

Speaking quietly and soothingly, Travers calmed down his horse and caught the reins. He found his hat, which had come off when he went flying out of the saddle. Then he mounted up, wincing as pain shot through his shoulder, and headed for Buckston's once more.

Who had reason to kill him? A lot of people might fit that description, but tonight there were only two logical answers.

Galen had found out somehow that he was going to warn Buckston. The rancher would want to stop that at all costs. Either that or Emory had returned to the ranch in time to be sent out on the killing errand. One of them had ridden hard and gotten in front of him to set up the ambush, Travers decided. It had to be that way.

Damn, but his shoulder was really starting to hurt now.

He knew from talking to the other hands on the UJ where Buckston's ranch was, but finding it in the dark with a wounded shoulder was another matter. Travers supposed he was due for a little luck, though, because he rode right to the place.

When he spotted the lights of the ranch house up ahead, he slowed the horse to a walk. Given the state of affairs in the valley, there was a good chance Buckston had guards posted.

Travers was still a quarter of a mile from the house when a man stepped out from behind a tree and leveled a rifle at him. "Hold on there," the guard snapped. "Who the hell are you, mister, and what do you want?"

Leaning forward in the saddle and trying not to pass out, Travers said hoarsely, "I've got to see Buckston."

"Keep your hands away from your gun." The guard stepped closer, holding the rifle in one hand and using the other to scratch a lucifer into blazing life against the seat of his pants. In the glare of the light, Travers saw a homely, beard-stubbled face peering up at him.

"Hell's fire!" the man exclaimed. "I recognize you, mister. You're the one kept us from stringin' up that damn rustler." The guard squinted as he saw the blood on Travers's shirt. "Who plugged ya?"

"Wish I knew," Travers grated. "Listen, I've got to talk to Buckston. Take my gun if you want to. Just get me to the house before I pass out."

The man reached up and slipped Travers's Colt out of its holster. As he tucked it behind his belt, he said, "Damn right I'll take your gun. I ain't just about to let one of that Englisher's hired killers anywhere near the boss 'thout pullin' his teeth." The guard jerked the barrel of the rifle toward the lights of the house. "Ride on slow. I'll be right behind you."

Travers did as he was told. The pain in his shoulder was beginning to subside again. He wasn't sure if that was a good sign or not.

When they were about fifty yards from the house, the guard sang out to let the men inside know they were coming. By the time Travers stopped his horse in front of the porch, several men had come out to greet him. One of them carried a lantern. The others all had guns.

Travers lifted his eyes and took in the scene. The house was a sturdy-looking frame structure, whitewashed and well cared for, surrounded by cottonwoods. A nice place to live, he thought irrelevantly. He knew that Buckston was a widower, but it looked like he had kept the place up since the death of his wife, instead of letting it go like a lot of men did in the same circumstances.

The ranch land he had passed through was fine, too. He was starting to understand why Buckston would want to fight for this place.

Forrest Buckston himself stood in the center of the porch and cradled a shotgun in his arms. As he stared at Travers, he said, "What the hell do you want, Travers?"

"Come to tell you . . . I was wrong," Travers got out.

And then he started to fall out of the saddle.

The guard dropped the rifle and caught him before he sprawled on the ground. Buckston whipped the shotgun around and barked, "Careful! Could be a trick!"

Travers was vaguely aware of the man supporting him saying, "I don't think so, boss. He's lost a lot of blood."

"Well, bring him on in the house," Buckston said disgustedly. "I don't like havin' his kind around, but I ain't goin' to let a man bleed to death in my front yard."

Travers felt himself being lifted and carried inside. He didn't pass out completely as he was placed in an armchair with a slicker draped over it to keep the blood off. Someone tore his shirt away from the wounded shoulder.

"Fetch the doc," Buckston ordered.

Travers heard the front door slam. A few minutes later, one of the hands knelt beside the chair and lifted a bottle to his mouth. "Drink some o' this," the man said.

Travers swallowed the whiskey, choked a little, drank some more. The man took the bottle away from his lips.

The liquor jolted warmth into his stomach. Travers blinked and looked up at the men surrounding him. There were still plenty of guns in evidence, but the men seemed more relaxed now, as if they had realized that he was no threat.

Buckston stood in front of him. He said harshly, "Who shot you, Travers?"

Travers lifted his head to look up at the old rancher. "Not sure," he replied slowly. "Reckon . . . it was either Galen Pritchard . . . or Emory Moore."

Buckston frowned. "You're one of Pritchard's men, and that Moore feller's supposed to be your friend. Why would either of them shoot you?"

"Because of something I found out." Travers felt stronger now as the whiskey took hold. One of the hands came out of the kitchen carrying a basin of hot water and a cloth. The man knelt beside the chair and began cleaning away the dried blood around the wound as Travers went on, "Can I talk to you in private, Buckston?"

For a long moment, Buckston considered the request, suspicion plain in his squinted eyes. Then he nodded abruptly. To the man cleaning the wound, he said, "When you're through there, Jase, go on back to the kitchen. The rest of you boys head on out to the bunkhouse. Find out what's keeping the doc."

Several of the punchers grumbled about being sent away, pointing out that Buckston shouldn't trust Travers. Buckston ignored them. When the two of them were alone in the room, the rancher went on, "All right, Travers. You've got a few minutes before the doc gets here."

"Figured the doctor was all the way in La Junta," Travers said.

Buckston shook his head. "You're a lucky son of a bitch. One of my men got his foot stepped on by a steer late this afternoon. Doc come out to tend to him and hadn't started back to town yet, far as I know. Now tell me what the devil this is all about."

Travers took a deep breath. He felt a little light-headed. Best to tell it straight out, he decided.

"Galen Pritchard's going to divert La Junta Creek so that it flows through the center of his land. Emory Moore killed Demeter so that Galen could get his hands on the place."

Buckston's eyes narrowed even more. He didn't say anything for a moment, and when he finally spoke, his voice was slow and deliberate. "If Pritchard messes with that creek, he'll ruin the rest of the valley."

Travers nodded. "I know."

"You know all this for a fact, about the creek and about Demeter bein' killed?"

"I saw the work at the springs where the creek starts. And I found Demeter's grave."

A muscle twitched in Buckston's cheek. Suddenly the man's

face looked almost gaunt. "When'd you find out about this?"

"Today," Travers told him. "After some of your men tried to kill me."

Buckston grimaced. "I never told the boys to kill nobody. They was just supposed to throw a scare into any of Pritchard's men they run across."

"Well, they came close to doing more than that. Don't reckon that matters much now, though. You've been wrong, Buckston, but Galen's done a lot worse. What he's planning is the worst yet."

Buckston turned to the wall and placed the shotgun on a rack there with several other weapons. "He's goin' to ruin a lot of good folks, drive 'em right off land they've worked and bled for. Reckon somebody's got to stop him."

"That's why I came here tonight."

Buckston shot a swift glance at him. "Since when did a gunhand like you get religion, Travers?"

Travers had to grin through the dull ache that was coming from his shoulder. He thought about old George and the run-down trading post at Ghost River. "I wouldn't call it religion," he said. "But I reckon sooner or later a man's got to take a stand for something. A friend taught me that."

Before either man could say anything else, the front door opened again and a portly, middle-aged man carrying a black bag hurried in. "Deke said there was a man shot up here, Buck," the doctor said. He gestured at Travers. "This the fella?"

Buckston snorted. "Naw, he's been bleedin' like that from a skeeter bite, you old pill-pusher. Of course he's the one!"

"Don't get your liver in an uproar," the doctor muttered. He bent over Travers and studied the bullet wound. "Yep. Shot, all right. Help me get this shirt all the way off of him."

Buckston stepped forward and helped lift Travers out of the chair while the doctor pulled the bloody shirt off. "How's Dave doin'?" the rancher asked.

"Not bad," the doctor grunted. "He won't lose the foot, I don't think, but he sure as hell don't need any cows stomping on it for a while." The shirt suddenly dropped from his fingers as he exclaimed, "My God!"

Travers looked at the doctor's startled face. "What is it?" he asked. "Am I hit somewhere else?"

The medico gazed at his torso with wide eyes. "That shoulder crease is nothing serious, just messy. But that—" He pointed at the big scars on Travers's body from the wound he had received at Grady. "That should have killed you!"

Travers suddenly remembered the reaction that Milburn Pritchard had shown when he saw the scars. This doctor looked equally startled, but he wasn't able to cover it up as Pritchard had done. "What are you saying, Doc?" he asked.

"What caliber of gun did that to you?" the doctor asked. Then, before Travers could answer, he told Buckston, "Let him sit back down, Buck."

As Travers settled in the chair, he said, "I don't rightly know what size cartridge it was; probably a .44 or a .45."

"Well, my friend, you shouldn't have any stomach left, for one thing. For another, the shock of being shot in the belly like that with a large-caliber bullet should have killed you within hours. Did you get medical attention right away?"

Travers shook his head. "Not until the middle of the night, and then it was just some sort of poultice that an old codger put on there."

The doctor still looked astounded. He said, "I don't know who that old codger was, but I'd say he worked a miracle. You must have a guardian angel, young man."

Travers thought about George again. He'd never seen an angel with tobacco juice dribbling into his whiskers. But hell, he'd never seen an angel of any kind, as far as he knew.

Buckston pointed at the fresh wound. "What about that shoulder?"

"Oh, that," the doctor shrugged. "I'll disinfect it and put a dressing on it. After that, the lad will need some sleep and some hot food, maybe some more whiskey. It'll be stiff for a few days, but it should be fine." He stared intently at Travers again. "Have you suffered any aftereffects from that other wound?"

"It was sore for a while," Travers told him. "But that's about all."

The doctor shook his head. "A miracle, plain and simple. A pure-dee miracle. . . ."

Travers didn't know about that. He gritted his teeth as the doctor cleaned the bullet crease and then taped a bandage over it. The medico left to take his buggy back to town, still shaking his head.

Buckston turned toward the kitchen as Travers leaned back in the chair. "I'll have the cook rustle you some grub," the rancher said.

"Buckston."

Travers's voice stopped the older man. He turned back. "Yeah?"

"What are you going to do about Galen?"

Buckston's face was grim. "Goin' to stop him. You know when he was planning to pull that business with the creek?"

"He'll be in a hurry now," Travers said. "He probably knows I came to you tonight. But there was still a little work to do before he'll be ready to dynamite the cut where the creek flows away from the springs. I'd say he won't be able to finish up until noon tomorrow, anyway."

"We'll be there before then," Buckston said flatly. "The boys and I will stop him."

"What about sending for the sheriff?"

"He'll be on his own land, even if he did have Demeter killed to get it. Reckon the law'd sort it all out sooner or later, but I ain't got time for that, Travers. Neither do all the other folks around here who depend on that creek."

Travers nodded. Buckston's answer didn't surprise him, and he couldn't say that he disagreed with it, either.

"I'm going," he said. "I'll be able to ride by morning."

For the first time, Travers saw something like friendship in Buckston's eyes.

"Figured you would," the old rancher said.

Chapter Sixteen

Travers tried not to wince as he mounted his horse. The shoulder was still sore and stiff this morning, as the doctor had said it would be, but he could use his left arm. More importantly, it wouldn't prevent him from riding.

"How're you doin'?" Buckston asked from beside him.

Travers nodded. "I'm fine," he declared.

He had slept better than he expected during what was left of the night before, aided considerably by several more slugs of the whiskey. His stomach had been a little queasy this morning, but he had been able to eat the breakfast prepared by Buckston's cook. He felt stronger now. A fresh bandage on his shoulder and a clean shirt had made him feel downright human again.

"Ready to ride?"

Again Travers nodded.

As he glanced at the men around him, he felt like he was about to go off to war. Well, that was what it amounted to, he supposed. Buckston had all of his men armed and mounted, and no doubt Galen would have plenty of help on hand at the springs.

Travers was glad the showdown was going to be taking place in those rugged foothills. Leanne and Milburn Pritchard would be out of harm's way at Galen's ranch.

Buckston lifted an arm. The burly old man was freshly shaved and wearing clean clothes. "Let's go!" he called, spurring his horse into a trot.

With the others, Travers fell in behind him.

They rode west toward the mountains, a group of silent, grim-faced men going out to defend everything that was dear to them. Travers understood them now, understood things that he never would have been able to fathom if he had kept on drifting and stealing.

This valley wasn't his, but he had a stake in the fight anyway.

As they moved onto the range that had once been Arthur Demeter's, Travers scanned the foothills and saw the thin haze of dust in the air above them. A lot of riders had been on the move up there.

There was a sudden rumble from the bench where the springs were located.

Buckston yanked his horse to a stop and glanced angrily at Travers. "Thought you said he couldn't be ready before noon!"

Travers shook his head. "Don't see how he could have been." He spurred his horse ahead. "Come on!"

They galloped harder now. Travers felt a sense of dread eating at him. Were they too late already?

They avoided the arroyo, taking another route up onto the bench. Travers let Buckston take the lead, since he knew the trails. As they came in sight of the springs, Travers heaved a sigh of relief. A plume of dust was still spiraling into the air from the arroyo, and he realized that Galen must have used some of the dynamite to make the work there go quicker.

Rifles began to crack from the timber at the back of the benchland.

Galen had men stationed there to protect the workers, Travers thought. He was expecting trouble.

Like a troop of cavalry, Buckston's men charged across the bench, whooping and firing.

As Travers emptied his Colt toward the trees, he saw men riding near him go tumbling and sprawling, flung out of their saddles by bullets. He felt a sick emptiness inside, a feeling like the one he had experienced back in Grady when he saw the splatter of blood on the wall behind the clerk.

Damn it, there should have been some way to stop this without getting so many people killed!

Too late for that now. All he could do was ride and shoot, reload, empty the weapon again—

He saw a wagon heading toward the cut where the creek flowed. The back of it was empty except for one crate. Two men were on the seat, one whipping the team on, the other firing a Winchester.

Emory and Galen.

The rifle in Emory's hand cracked, and the bullet whined over Travers's head. They had spotted him, Travers knew. He veered his horse in that direction.

Galen was going to blow the cut, even if all the other work wasn't quite done.

The gunfire continued behind Travers as he headed after the wagon. The thought raced through his mind that everyone else might as well stop fighting. The important confrontation was about to take place up ahead, where the creek began its journey into the valley.

Buckston and his men, the hands from the UJ—all they were doing was wasting bullets and lives.

Travers wanted to turn in his saddle and scream at them to stop, but he knew it wouldn't do any good. He just hoped that not too many of them would get killed because of Galen Pritchard's ambition.

Emory was still shooting at him. The wagon had almost reached the gash in the earth now. Galen hauled back on the lines, bringing the vehicle to a lurching stop. With Emory covering him, he hopped into the back of the wagon and lifted the crate of dynamite.

Travers snapped a shot at him, missing. Emory stood up on the wagon seat and levered the Winchester. The rifle blasted again, and Travers heard the awful thump as the slug took his horse in the chest.

The animal didn't even cry out in pain. It just went down, head over heels. Travers kicked loose from the stirrups and flung himself desperately to the side. An image of the fall he had taken on Colonel Jeb Stuart flashed through his mind, and then he slammed into the ground.

His hand was empty, he suddenly realized. He had dropped his gun.

Gasping for breath, he lifted his head and looked frantically for the weapon. It had fallen several feet to his right. He came up on one knee and started to lunge toward the Colt.

A bullet smacked into the dirt in front of him.

"Hold it, Jacob!" Emory called.

Travers looked up. Emory had the Winchester lined up on his head. Beyond him, Galen was wrestling the crate of explosives into position against one of the overhanging banks of the cut.

"I never did wish you any harm, Jacob," Emory said. "You were a good man to ride with, a good partner."

Travers drew a ragged breath. He could still hear the popping of guns up at the springs, but the firing seemed to be slacking off.

"But you'll kill me anyway, won't you?" Travers said harshly. "I know you murdered Demeter, so you've got to shut me up. You tried hard enough last night."

Emory grinned. "That's right, Jacob. You didn't see me, but I got back to the ranch in time to hear you talkin' to that English gal. Won't do to have you tellin' stories on me. I'd've had you last night if you hadn't gotten lucky and bounced a slug off my rifle." He chuckled, but his eyes behind the spectacles were cold. "Leastways I put one more over on you with that rope and those rattles. Damn, I never seen a man jump like you did that day. Funniest thing I ever saw."

"The joke's on you this time, Emory," Travers said with a shake of his head. "I'm not the only one who knows about you and Demeter. Buckston knows, too, and so does Galen's father."

"Who'll believe Buckston, even if he lives through this fightin'? Once Pritchard's got the creek to himself, nobody in these parts will dare cross him. And he can handle the old man, don't worry about that."

Travers recognized the truth of that. Galen would have too much money, too much power, to ever be stopped.

Behind Emory, Galen straightened from his task and called, "It's ready! Kill him!" He pulled matches from his pocket and bent over the fuse.

Travers threw himself toward his gun. Hopeless or not, he had to try. . . .

His fingers slapped the butt of the Colt as Emory's Winchester blasted. Travers lifted the gun, not bothering to aim, and fired twice as his stomach thumped into the ground.

Emory's head snapped back, splinters of glass sparkling in the morning sun as the bullets shattered his spectacles. He staggered back against the horses that were hitched to the wagon. The team bolted, driven out of their heads by the shots and the smell of blood.

The corner of the wagon clipped Emory as it bounced by, spinning him around. He pitched forward on his face, the rifle slipping from his hands, and Travers could see the back of Emory's ruined head where both bullets had exited.

Travers put a hand on the ground, pushed himself up. His shoulder wound had started bleeding again, but other than that he seemed to be all right.

Emory's shot had missed.

Hell of a joke, all right. Travers thought bitterly.

Galen Pritchard leaped toward the wagon as the team careened past him. Travers saw the fuse, cut too short in Galen's haste, sputtering behind him, closing in on the open crate of dynamite. Galen misjudged his leap, and the shoulder of one of the horses smacked into him, knocking him down.

Both wheels on the right side of the wagon rolled over his foot. He screamed.

There wasn't a damn thing Travers could do.

He threw himself down again as the dynamite went off with an ear-jarring boom. The ground shook under him, and dirt and rocks showered down around him.

He wasn't sure how long he stayed that way, but the next thing he knew, someone was holding his arm in a strong grip and was lifting him. He blinked dust out of his eyes and looked into the face of Forrest Buckston.

Buckston jerked his chin toward the site of the explosion. "Pritchard?" he asked. All the shooting seemed to be over, and the hillside was strangely quiet.

Travers looked at the mound of earth where the bank of the cut had collapsed, damming up the flow of the creek. What was left of Galen Pritchard was lying nearby. A little closer was the sprawled body of Emory Moore. On the far side of the cut, the wagon had been blown on its side, and the horses, cut by the flying debris, were thrashing and screaming.

Travers watched the water backing up and then beginning to trickle toward the waiting arroyo.

"Galen got what he wanted," he said.

Travers knew he was a grimy, bloody sight as he rode up the UJ ranch house a couple of hours later. He was too tired to care.

Buckston rode on one side of him, the sheriff from La Junta on the other. They had swung by the town to get the lawman on their way to the UJ. He had had plenty of questions, and Travers figured that none of them were through with hashing this out yet. But that could wait for the time being.

Now there was another errand to take care of.

Behind him were Buckston's men, the ones who hadn't been hurt bad enough to leave behind in town. Galen Pritchard's cowboys rode with them, Galen's men disarmed for the moment. Travers didn't think they would give any more trouble, though, not after the explosive end to the battle of La Junta Creek.

Miraculously, no one had been killed in the fighting except Galen and Emory, although there were plenty of assorted bullet holes to be patched up. Or maybe it wasn't so miraculous,

Travers mused. After all, these men were cowhands, not gunfighters. He and Emory had been the only ones who were even close to being professional gunmen, and they'd been busy shooting at each other.

Leanne must have been waiting and watching. As they rode up to the house, the iron gate into the patio opened and she came out, her pale face showing the strain she was feeling.

Behind her, looking even more haggard, came Dr. Milburn Pritchard.

As the group of riders drew their mounts to a halt, Leanne came to Travers's horse and put a hand on his leg. "Are you all right?" she asked.

He nodded and slowly dismounted. Looking past her at Pritchard, Travers did just about the hardest thing he had ever come up against.

"I've got something to tell both of you," he said.

Chapter Seventeen

"Are you sure I can't convince you to stay?" Milburn Pritchard asked.

Travers shook his head as he swung up into the saddle. "I appreciate the offer, Doc, but I'm afraid I wouldn't ever feel comfortable here. Besides, there's something I've got to do." He looked over at the buggy. Leanne was on the seat, the reins in her hand. "You ready?"

She nodded, a faint smile on her face.

Funny how quickly things could change, Travers thought. Sometimes they changed for the worse . . . but every now and then they were put right again.

Almost a week had passed since the showdown with Galen and Emory. Up in the hills, work was well under way to restore the creek to its original course. Milburn Pritchard, once he had recovered from the initial shock of his son's death, had readily given his permission for the project. A crew made up of hands from both the UJ and Buckston's ranch were carrying out the work. There was an uneasy truce between the men now that they all knew how Galen had acquired the springs in the first place. As far as the authorities were concerned, the sale of the Demeter place was legal. The finding of Demeter's body wasn't evidence that the contracts had been signed at gunpoint. But everyone in the valley knew what had actually happened, and the sheriff was willing to turn a blind eye to the fact that Buckston and his men had been trespassing during their battle with the UJ hands.

At first, Travers knew, Milburn Pritchard had hated him and blamed him for Galen's death. But that had slowly changed as the truth of the situation sank in on him. As Galen's only living relative, ownership of the ranch had gone to him, and Forrest Buckston had paid him a visit, hoping to ensure peace in the future between the two spreads.

Travers had a feeling things were going to be all right now. Pritchard and Buckston had gotten along once the tension between them had relaxed a little.

Pritchard had even surprised Travers by asking him to stay on and help him run the ranch. Travers had had to think about that one; it had been a long time since he'd had a place to call home. But in the end, he had decided that there were just too many memories here to haunt him.

Besides, Leanne didn't want to stay, and that played a part in his decision, too.

He didn't know how things would turn out between the two of them. They were going to travel together for a while, though, and see how it went.

They were a lot alike, Travers thought. He had his hopes. . . .

Milburn Pritchard broke into his reverie by lifting his hand. "Well, if I can't persuade you to change your mind, at least I can wish you good luck and Godspeed, my boy."

Travers shook his head. "Thanks, Doc. Maybe we'll be back this way sometime."

"I probably won't be here," Pritchard said with a smile. "Once I've put everything right, I may see about selling this place and taking the medicine wagon back on the road again. As a doctor, I feel a certain responsibility to give the good folks of this territory the opportunity to purchase the finest elixir ever known to man, the most healthful tonic ever produced—"

Leanne slapped the reins on the back of the horse hitched to the buggy. "Let's go," she said to Travers with a grin, "before he really gets started."

Travers touched the brim of his hat in farewell and then wheeled his horse to fall in beside the buggy. He didn't look back.

"Which way?" Leanne asked a moment later, as they left the ranch house behind them.

"North," Travers said. "Like I told the doc, I've got something to do."

Leanne glanced up at him. "I thought you were a man who liked to just drift."

Travers nodded ruefully. "Reckon that's true. But I'm tired of having things hanging over my head. I'm going back to Grady."

"The place where you shot that man in the robbery?" Leanne sounded surprised.

"That's right."

"But won't they put you in jail?" The dismay was plain in Leanne's voice.

"Probably. But maybe they won't hang me." Travers tried to sound hopeful. "However it turns out, it's something I've got to do."

He had reached that decision during the days following the fight at the springs. He'd been running away all his life, until here lately. He didn't want to start that pattern all over again.

Travers just hoped he wasn't making the biggest damn-fool mistake of his life.

After a couple of days on the trail, he started looking for landmarks.

"What's wrong?" Leanne asked from the buggy. "We're not getting close to Grady yet, are we?"

Travers shook his head. "Nope. But we ought to be getting to that river I told you about."

"Ghost River?"

"Right. I thought I'd stop by the trading post and see that old man who saved my life. I'd still like to find out what that remedy of his was. The doctor from La Junta said I should have died from that bullet wound."

"You're a lucky man, Jacob. Sometimes that can be more important than any kind of medicine."

She had a point there. And Travers realized that maybe she was right about him being lucky. Things could have turned out a whole hell of a lot worse for him. For the first time in years, he had a future to look forward to.

Maybe.

"I just don't understand it!" he exclaimed a little later. He had spotted some familiar hills, and now they were paused on top of a rise which should have overlooked the river and trading post. He remembered this spot. He had watched the posse from here.

Down below there was nothing. No river, no trading post. Just a dusty stretch of ground dotted with scrubby mesquites and cactus.

He pointed. "The river should be right there, with the trading post beside it. Dammit, I know I'm not lost!"

Leanne studied him with concern on her face. Gently, she said, "You were wounded, Jacob. Perhaps you simply . . . imagined it."

Travers shook his head. "I wasn't seeing things."

Leanne tried to smile. "Well, the stream was called Ghost River. Perhaps the elderly gentleman at the trading post was a ghost himself."

Travers glared at the emptiness where the river should have been. He started to wonder if he had gone crazy. Maybe this memory was playing tricks on him. Maybe they weren't even in the right place.

"Don't move, you son of a bitch!"

The voice came from behind Travers, sharp and commanding.

There was something familiar about it, something that made his blood go icy.

Leanne gasped. Travers heard the ominous click of a hammer being drawn back, and he said quickly, "Sit still, Leanne. They mean business."

Slowly, he turned his head and looked over his shoulder, keeping his hands half raised so as not to spook anybody. Emerging from their place of concealment behind a clump of brush were three men. The one who had spoken was young and blond, and his face was twisted with hate.

"I knew I'd catch up to you again, mister," Dale Sorenson said, his voice shaking with emotion. The barrel of the gun in his hand was rock-steady, though.

Travers kept his face and his voice tightly controlled. "Reckon those are two more of your brothers," he said.

"That's right," one of the other men grated as he pointed a massive Dragoon pistol at Travers. "It was my boy that quack medicine man killed with his tonic."

Travers knew talking wouldn't do any good, but he had to try. "Doc Pritchard didn't kill your boy, mister. It was just pure bad luck."

"Shut up! You killed Coley and Bramwell, you bastard, so we got a score to even with you, too!"

They had to be stopped, Travers knew. They weren't going to be talked out of their revenge. It was just chance that had led to this meeting, but if the Sorensons were allowed to continue on their way, they would run right into Milburn Pritchard at the UJ.

Even with the hands to back him up, Pritchard would probably wind up dead.

And what about Leanne? It had been obvious the first time some of the Sorensons caught up to the medicine wagon that they intended to rape and kill her. It wouldn't be any different now.

But there were three of them, Travers thought bleakly, and they had the drop on him. If he went for his gun, he might manage to down one of them, but the other two would riddle him.

Dale Sorenson wore an ugly grin as he moved a step closer.

177

"Couldn't believe it when we spotted you coming, mister," he said. "I told 'em it was you, so we hid and let you ride right into our laps. Reckon all your luck ran out."

As his lips drew back in a grimace of fury, Dale Sorenson raised his gun, his finger whitening on the trigger.

Travers saw the moving shadow out of the corner of his eye, heard the flapping of leathery wings as the buzzard seemed to drop down out of a clear blue sky. The ugly bird's talons raked Dale Sorenson's neck as it glanced off him, knocking him to the side.

Travers dropped out of the saddle, twisting to face the men as he fell. He landed on one knee. The Colt slid smoothly out of its holster and bucked against his palm as he triggered it.

The buzzard screeched and flapped away awkwardly, startled by the thunder of gunfire. Dale Sorenson was thrown backward by the bullet smacking into his chest. Before he hit the ground, Travers had fired twice more. Those two slugs knocked the remaining Sorenson brothers off their feet.

Travers stayed where he was for a long moment, holding the gun ready in case there was any movement from the three sprawled bodies. When it became obvious there wasn't going to be, he straightened from his crouch and walked slowly over to them.

All three of them were dead. He didn't even know the names of the older brothers, but he had killed them all the same. He rammed his Colt back in the holster and took a deep breath, then looked up to see where the buzzard had gone.

It was nowhere to be seen. It had flown back high into the sky, Travers thought, where it had come from in the first place. He had seen buzzards dive like that before, but never at anything alive.

He turned and walked back to the buggy. Leanne was still sitting on the seat, her face pale and drawn. "It's over," Travers told her, reaching out to lay a hand on her arm.

She drew a ragged breath. "I . . . I thought they were going to kill us."

"So did I." Travers tried to smile, but he didn't make a very good job of it.

"If that . . . that bird hadn't come out of nowhere . . ."

Travers didn't say anything. If he was going to be crazy, Travers thought, might as well go whole hog.

He had recognized that buzzard. Lucky though its timing had been for them, it hadn't come out of nowhere.

The last time he had seen it, it had been inside the Ghost River Trading Post . . . with old George.

A guardian angel. That was what the doctor from La Junta had said.

Well, Travers thought, maybe. Just maybe.

Epilogue

The town of Grady was still about as sun-blasted a place as Jacob Travers had ever seen. There were plenty of people on the streets today, because this was Saturday afternoon, the high point of the week for the ranch folks around here.

And this time Travers expected every one of them to recognize him and point an accusing finger at him.

He rode slowly down the street, Leanne in the buggy beside him. He nodded toward the mercantile and express office. "That's where it happened," he said in a low voice.

"Do you think you'll be arrested?" she asked. She was trying not to show her concern, but Travers knew how worried she was. Neither of them had said the words yet, but they both knew how they were starting to feel. He had been an outlaw and she had been what some people would consider a whore, and neither of them had been very good at what they did.

Together, they might have a chance for something better.

"I'm going to turn myself in at the sheriff's office," he said now. "I expect he'll lock me up. There's something I want to do first, though."

He rode up to the express office and dismounted, finding a place at the hitch rail to tie his horse. Leanne brought the buggy to a stop nearby. Travers helped her down. With his hand on her arm, they climbed the steps onto the sidewalk and went to the door of the express office.

The mercantile was busy, as usual, Travers saw, but the express office itself only had a couple of customers at the moment. He didn't know why he felt compelled to see the place again, but there was no denying it. He had to revisit the scene of his first killing.

With Leanne beside him, he stepped through the door.

And stopped short as he saw the clerk behind the counter.

The man was waiting on one of the customers. Travers tried not to gawk. It was the same clerk, no doubt about that, looking hale and hearty.

"Jacob?" Leanne whispered.

He shook his head. "Stay here," he told her.

When the customer turned away from the counter, Travers stepped up, expecting to see a flash of recognition and anger in the clerk's eyes. Instead, there was only a little bored interest as the man said, "Can I help you?"

Travers tried to find words. "Ah . . . was there a holdup here at this express office awhile back?"

The question sparked a reaction in the clerk. He grinned and replied, "You bet there was. Quite a shoot-out, too. I got a little scratch myself."

"A little scratch?" Travers choked out.

The clerk nodded. "Got plugged in the arm. Just a nick, really. It bled some, but I'm good as new now." His grin widened and he lowered his voice. "I tell you, mister, the gals in this town got right friendly once word got around that I was a hero. I never had so many ladies fussing over me until I got shot by that desperado."

"What happened to the outlaws?" Travers managed to ask.

"Oh, we killed three of 'em right here in town. The other one, the one who winged me, he got away, but I heard tell later that he got killed down south a ways."

Travers was having a hard time getting his breath. He said, "The fella who shot you—what did he look like?"

"Ugly son of a gun. Looked a little like a farmer. He wore thick spectacles. I remember that."

Travers gave a little shake of his head. "What about the fifth man?"

The clerk frowned. "What fifth man? There were only four of them, and I ought to know, mister. I was right here, after all." The man leaned his palms on the counter. He had obviously enjoyed jawing about the robbery and his newfound status as a hero, but he had a job to do. "Now, can I help you with something? You have a shipment you need sent out?"

Travers lifted a hand, shook his head, and backed away from the window. The clerk frowned after him as if he thought Travers was some kind of lunatic.

He took Leanne's arm. "What is it?" she asked.

"Let's go," he told her. "We're not staying after all."

She smiled up at him. "I'm glad, Jacob. I'm very glad."

They rode out of Grady, heading north. Travers didn't know where they would wind up.

As long as they were together, he didn't care.

Maybe he was crazy, Travers thought. He remembered all the strange things that had happened since he had ridden away from Grady with a bullet hole in his belly—from old George and his vanishing trading post to a buzzard who came out of nowhere just when he was needed.

Travers decided suddenly that he wasn't going to ask any more questions. Not a damn one. . . .